ALWAYS, WITH YOU

(Endless harbor—BOOK 1)

FIONA GRACE

Fiona Grace

Fiona Grace is author of the LACEY DOYLE COZY MYSTERY series, comprising nine books; of the TUSCAN VINEYARD COZY MYSTERY series, comprising seven books; of the DUBIOUS WITCH COZY MYSTERY series, comprising three books; of the BEACHFRONT BAKERY COZY MYSTERY series, comprising six books; of the CATS AND DOGS COZY MYSTERY series, comprising nine books; of the ELIZA MONTAGU COZY MYSTERY series, comprising five books (and counting); and of the ENDLESS HARBOR ROMANTIC COMEDY series, comprising five books (and counting).

Fiona would love to hear from you, so please visit www.fionagraceauthor.com to receive free ebooks, hear the latest news, and stay in touch.

BOOKS BY FIONA GRACE

ENDLESS HARBOR ROMANTIC COMEDY
ALWAYS, WITH YOU (Book #1)
ALWAYS, FOREVER (Book #2)
ALWAYS, PLUS ONE (Book #3)
ALWAYS, TOGETHER (Book #4)
ALWAYS, LIKE THIS (Book #5)

ELIZA MONTAGU COZY MYSTERY
MURDER AT THE HEDGEROW (Book #1)
A DALLOP OF DEATH (Book #2)
CALAMITY AT THE BALL (Book #3)
A SPEAKEASY DEMISE (Book #4)
A FLAPPER FATALITY (Book #5)

LACEY DOYLE COZY MYSTERY
MURDER IN THE MANOR (Book#1)
DEATH AND A DOG (Book #2)
CRIME IN THE CAFE (Book #3)
VEXED ON A VISIT (Book #4)
KILLED WITH A KISS (Book #5)
PERISHED BY A PAINTING (Book #6)
SILENCED BY A SPELL (Book #7)
FRAMED BY A FORGERY (Book #8)
CATASTROPHE IN A CLOISTER (Book #9)

TUSCAN VINEYARD COZY MYSTERY
AGED FOR MURDER (Book #1)
AGED FOR DEATH (Book #2)
AGED FOR MAYHEM (Book #3)
AGED FOR SEDUCTION (Book #4)
AGED FOR VENGEANCE (Book #5)
AGED FOR ACRIMONY (Book #6)
AGED FOR MALICE (Book #7)

DUBIOUS WITCH COZY MYSTERY
SKEPTIC IN SALEM: AN EPISODE OF MURDER (Book #1)
SKEPTIC IN SALEM: AN EPISODE OF CRIME (Book #2)

SKEPTIC IN SALEM: AN EPISODE OF DEATH (Book #3)

BEACHFRONT BAKERY COZY MYSTERY
BEACHFRONT BAKERY: A KILLER CUPCAKE (Book #1)
BEACHFRONT BAKERY: A MURDEROUS MACARON (Book #2)
BEACHFRONT BAKERY: A PERILOUS CAKE POP (Book #3)
BEACHFRONT BAKERY: A DEADLY DANISH (Book #4)
BEACHFRONT BAKERY: A TREACHEROUS TART (Book #5)
BEACHFRONT BAKERY: A CALAMITOUS COOKIE (Book #6)

CATS AND DOGS COZY MYSTERY
A VILLA IN SICILY: OLIVE OIL AND MURDER (Book #1)
A VILLA IN SICILY: FIGS AND A CADAVER (Book #2)
A VILLA IN SICILY: VINO AND DEATH (Book #3)
A VILLA IN SICILY: CAPERS AND CALAMITY (Book #4)
A VILLA IN SICILY: ORANGE GROVES AND VENGEANCE (Book #5)
A VILLA IN SICILY: CANNOLI AND A CASUALTY (Book #6)

CHAPTER ONE

"Quite frankly, Ms. Hawthorne, we're ready to move forward on this with or without your approval."

The amount of red that Ariel Hawthorne saw as those words rolled contemptuously out in the haughty voice of Opulent Ice's owner was fitting for today's winter board meeting—too bad that warm, fuzzy thoughts were not the first things that rose in her mind as the older man across from her delivered the message.

Ariel felt the eyes of a dozen people on her—Opulent Ice's CEO, the board members, even the secretary tasked with keeping the meeting minutes stared. The entire room plunged into awkward silence as those gathered watched, waiting to see what her reaction to Jim's patronizing tone would be.

She purposefully kept her voice even, focusing on the Opulent boardroom instead of Jim's face. Elegant modern décor. Long, mirror-polished marble conference table. Vintage local art gracing the walls. The wall of windows at the far end of the room that gave a breathtaking afternoon view of downtown Miami. She got the impression that Jim Chambers wanted her to snap back, but she wouldn't give him the satisfaction. She would be as Zen as the waves lapping at the sandy curves of the South Beach shore.

"Well, Mr. Chambers, as much as I admire your boldness, I have to ask why OI is making such a strategically unwise move. Our brand has always been associated with luxury, and the test kitchen is state-of-the-art to make sure that customers can get 'a five-star plate without the wait.' But if we're lowering those standards ..."

He laughed. It wasn't a pleasant sound.

"We *are* giving the customer what they want—value. In case you haven't noticed, consumers are increasingly savvy about where their dollars are going in the grocery space."

Ariel snatched up the report that was on the long, marble meeting table in front of her. She waved it as she stood. "Value at the sacrifice of quality. Why are we importing our seafood instead of sourcing it locally? It travels how far, and then has to go through packaging, and

1

transport, and then to the consumer? There are hundreds of fisheries in Florida. Ones we already have vendor relationships with. You're just going to stop doing business with them?"

Beside her on the conference table, Ariel's phone vibrated softly. Then, a moment later, it buzzed again two more times. Her stress heightened slightly—three messages? It could be Katie texting with some emergency. But there was no way she could check her texts in the middle of a board meeting—not without giving Jim more fuel for his vendetta against her.

Unprofessional, she could almost hear him say.

Jim steepled his fingers under his chin, his eyes glittering with malice that was at odds with his sudden, wide smile. She had never liked that smile. Not when she'd first met him twenty years ago as a snarky kid, and not when he'd taken over Opulent when his father had passed a few years back. "Ariel. When you came to Opulent, we were excited about your experience. I mean, the amount of press that you got while cooking in France—in just a few short years—was remarkable. And you've done fantastic work with the product development team—"

"Leading."

"Excuse me?" Jim's smile wavered as he swung his gaze over to the CEO, who had interrupted.

Riley Weston's voice was strong, confident, and serious. Everything that Ari had come to know about him over the past years of working with the man. His salt-and-pepper crew cut, his ramrod straight posture, his perfectly tailored suits—Riley was the picture of polish. He commanded attention and, to Jim's very apparent annoyance, respect in any room.

"Not just *with* the PD team, Jim. Ariel has led it for the past eighteen of those twenty years. You might remember that she joined when you were, oh, probably in middle school, I think?"

The barb didn't go unnoticed, but Jim only nodded shortly. The room was still holding its collective breath.

"I'm glad you brought that up, Riley. If you'll all turn to page six, let's discuss what the numbers have been for Ariel's tenure here. Especially the past two."

The sound of a dozen-plus paper reports flipping in the hush set Ariel's teeth on edge. Riley cut his eyes over to her, and a momentary expression of sympathy flickered over his patrician features.

It's okay, she wanted to say. *I've battled tougher than Jim Chambers.* As Jim began to call out profit margins and supply costs, Ariel almost smiled, remembering her first year in Paris, when a

2

mercurial sous chef had thrown a frying pan full of escargots at her. She'd stepped into his position three months later and then head chef three months after that. She wasn't scared of little ol' Legacy Jim.

Sales had been slipping, sure, but the mismanaging heir apparent was looking for a scapegoat, not a solution. It was completely and utterly unfair that *she* was apparently the one he was trying to lead to the slaughter.

She stood her ground.

"This isn't what your father would have wanted," she said resolutely. "And it isn't what I signed up for. There must be a compromise."

Jim's face began to mottle and then flush fully. Ariel held her breath, waiting for the outburst that would finally show the board—on full display—what the spoiled new owner of Opulent Ice was *really* like. But he didn't rise to her bait, either. Instead, he cut her line completely.

Taking a deep, slow breath and letting it out, Jim reached up, straightened his tie, and rolled back from the conference table slightly.

"You're right," he said. The whole room seemed to release their breath. "This isn't what you signed up for. So, I think it's time we re-evaluate that. As far as I am concerned, Opulent needs a Vice President of Product Development who is onboard with the on-trend momentum of the new ownership."

Ariel almost laughed out loud—was he really talking about *himself* in such glowing corporate-speak?

"What does that even *mean*?" she scoffed.

Jim's sharklike smile reappeared. "Effective immediately, Ms. Hawthorne, you're fired."

CHAPTER TWO

Reeling from what had transpired in the boardroom, Ariel fumbled with her phone as she power-walked down the hall to her office. She couldn't get to her emails or texts.

Her tight French twist suddenly felt too tight, her contact lenses dry and scratchy, and her head ached. She wanted to rip out all of her hair pins and let her long, dark hair down, trade her contacts for her big, clunky, black-framed glasses, and have a long, hot bath and a good cry.

Two hours.

That was all she had to pack her things and be out of the corner suite that had been her work home for two decades. And now, her phone was acting up. For the tenth time, she stabbed at the messages icon, only to have her screen flicker and throw her right back to the home screen.

No, no, no!

As she reached the door to her office, she swiped her access card and waited for the green light. The card scanner beeped twice and then remained red. Frowning, Ariel swiped her card again, only to have the scanner repeat the curious glitch.

Then realization dawned on her. It wasn't a glitch—Jim had already had her security access revoked. After ten minutes of pacing in the hallway and trying, still unsuccessfully, to load her text messages, Ariel called down to security to have someone come up to let her into her office.

Bruno from security came up within minutes, with a sheepish look on his face that was at odds with his burly stature. It wasn't often that the six-four former Marine looked anything but stoic and wall-like. The puppy dog eyes were a bit incongruous. And the empty cardboard box in his hand both confirmed her suspicions about Jim *and* spiked her anger higher.

"Ma'am," Bruno said to Ariel as he swiped her in, stepping in after her. She marched ahead of him, simmering. She thought that, with the way she felt right now, she might be able to take on the company bouncer—even though the top of her head barely came up to his chin.

But it wasn't Bruno's fault that the boss was a jerk.

"I'm fine here," she clipped out as she snatched the box that Bruno held out and stalked to her desk.

"I have orders to stay here with you until you're finished." Bruno checked his watch, and Ariel had to check herself. It wasn't as though she could argue with the block wall of a man standing in her doorway. Even if he did look like he was an unwilling participant in this little corporate coup.

Grumbling to herself, Ariel slammed the box onto her desk and dialed her daughter, putting the call on speaker.

Katie answered on the second ring, sounding dejected. "Hi, Mom."

"Katiebug, you okay? I can't get my messages, so I might have missed some of yours. You home yet?"

"Yep, I'm home. And I'm fine. Just a bad day."

Ariel began packing up her laptop, side-eyeing Bruno. "Yeah, kiddo, me too."

Bruno gave her a watery, sympathetic smile.

Her phone buzzed again, and she could see that message notifications were starting to flood in. But when she clicked on any of them, they simply vanished, not linking to the actual message. She sighed. "I'm going to have to let you go. I'll be home soon, okay? You want to use the delivery app to get pizza?"

Katie's voice brightened. "You're coming home now? Awesome! Can we watch that new DVD concert? It came in the mail today."

"Of course, sweetie. And, hey, throw some brownies in with that pizza order, will you?"

Katie happily agreed, and Ariel hung up smiling softly, despite the emotional cloud hanging over her. Her daughter never failed to be a bright spot in her day—and even on bad days when neither of them was sunny, they had each other to lean on.

As she packed the important things from her desk, Ariel restarted her phone. To her delight, the message icon dinged happily and counted up to several message notifications and then actually let her into her messages. There was one from a few hours ago from Dylan, asking how her day was going. She felt guilty that she hadn't seen it before the board meeting, so she fired off a quick text to him.

Awful day. Guess who is now unemployed? Please tell me you have something planned for the birthday of your stressed-out girlfriend that will take us far, far away from Miami. I'm thinking somewhere with the last snow of winter, and a storybook downtown, and no frozen food or legal briefs for an entire two weeks.

Ariel pictured Dylan in his office, or maybe in the courtroom, his handsome face and dreamy, blue eyes, the way he would captivate a courtroom. *Sigh.* She really hoped that he had planned something for her birthday because—she realized guiltily—she hadn't much thought about the event.

Ariel vaguely recalled brushing off her sister's invite to come back to Maine. "If you're taking time off for your birthday," Charlene had said, but Ariel had assumed she'd be working through it. Now, the last thing she wanted was to think about work.

The second message was from Katie, telling Ariel that she was catching a ride home with one of her friends from school. It was followed by a string of emoji texts and then a message telling Ariel that Katie was, indeed, home, and not "ax murdered on the mean streets of Miami." Ariel laughed at the teen dramatics and dismissed the message.

The last in the string of texts was unexpected. The number wasn't stored in her phone, but Ariel recognized the area code from one in Maine—back home, she always thought of it, even though she had been in Florida all these years. She read the text.

Ms. Hawthorne, this is Richard Holcomb from Holcomb and Associates. I know we haven't spoken in a few years, but I would like to speak with you in regard to your family's old estate in Endless Harbor. Please give me a call at your convenience. This is my direct line.

Ah, Holcomb. Round spectacles, tweed suit, and the same nervous disposition as he'd had in all the years that he had been the Hawthorne family attorney. It really had been years since she'd seen or spoken with him. Ariel dismissed this, as well, not willing to deal with anything related to the rickety, old Victorian that she'd grown up in. She wanted idyllic snowscapes and gingerbread of the fresh-baked variety, not the kind that was crumbling and falling off of the facia of a sagging, old front porch.

Besides, what would Richard Holcomb have to talk to *her* about, as far as Leeside was concerned? The old house—and its cutesy nickname—belonged to her sister, Charlie. He must have called Ariel by mistake.

Satisfied that she had everything that was vital, and informing Bruno that she would be sending a moving company for her furniture and other items, Ariel exited the building with as much grace as she could, having to walk out to her car accompanied by the tank-like security guard. At least Bruno had offered to carry her cardboard box.

Unexpectedly, once they reached her sedan and Bruno had loaded her belongings into the trunk, he gave her a tight bear hug and said, "Sorry, Ms. H. This ain't right." Then he turned and strode away quickly—but not before she saw the misty shine in his eyes.

"Thank you, Bruno!" she called after him, and he waved a meaty hand in the air but kept walking.

In her car alone, Ariel felt her own eyes finally fill too. She cried all the way home, so upset that she barely noticed the traffic that would normally be the source of her evening stress. When she pulled into the driveway of her sprawling Mediterranean Revival, she made sure to tidy her makeup so that it wasn't *so* apparent that she had been crying. She would be strong so that, when she broke the news to Katie, her daughter wouldn't feel like everything was out of control.

"Katie, I'm home!" Ariel called as she unlocked the door and pushed inside, balancing the carboard box. The smell of pizza wafted into the foyer, coming from the kitchen. Ariel rounded the corner into the open kitchen and family room to find Katie seated at the big, marble kitchen island.

Katie didn't wait until Ariel set down the box of stuff from her office—she launched at her mother, and Ariel caught her in an awkward side-hug with one arm, almost losing the contents of the box as the girl burst into tears. Words ran out in a near-unintelligible stream.

"I had a terrible day at school. Brittney and her minions are just getting *worse*. I'm never going back, and please don't make me. Mom, *please*."

Surprised, Ariel scooted over to the island, dragging Katie with her, half-patting her back as she slid the cardboard box onto the island. In the box, Ariel's phone dinged with a new message alert. Ariel picked it up as she scooped Katie into a full hug, making soothing shushing noises. She let her daughter cry into her shoulder, waiting it out.

Over Katie's shoulder, Ariel opened the screen for her messages. Maybe it would be Dylan, with some uplifting birthday getaway planned that would help both Ariel and Katie get over this awful day.

But it wasn't.

Ariel gaped at the phone screen. "You've got to be kidding me."

The text was from Dylan, but it wasn't anywhere near about mistletoe and ski slopes. It simply said:

This just isn't working out. It seems like we're going in different directions, and I need to focus on myself. Please respect my decision to end our relationship.

CHAPTER THREE

Ariel felt as though her entire life was falling apart—well, at least, that she had been robbed of having any input in Dylan's decision to break things off. And she *certainly* felt that she should have a say in the end of a three-year relationship. She *was* going to talk to Dylan, whether he liked it or not.

But first, she had a good, old-fashioned pity party. And Katie joined in. They spent all of Friday night watching sappy romcoms and teen dramas, polishing off a supreme pizza and an order of brownies, and making fresh, hot, buttery popcorn to share until they were both stuffed and drowsy. They talked about all of the day's disasters, and Ariel had to rein herself in from interrupting their mother-daughter evening to make a few angry phone calls to parents she'd talked with before— obviously to no effect. And, needless to say, she had to stop herself from texting or calling Dylan. She left him on "read," letting him sweat about her response.

"I can't believe him," Katie said as they sat on the couch, Ariel having just finished braiding Katie's long, brown hair. Their second romcom was rolling into the credits. Katie's tone held all the vitriol appropriate to a fifteen-year-old commiserating with a heartbroken friend. "He will never find anyone as awesome as you, Mom. He'll be lonely and come running right back."

Ariel laughed, patting Katie on the arm. As ferocious as her daughter sounded, Ariel was glad that Katie hadn't yet had her own heart broken. It was not a rite of passage that Ariel was looking forward to for her one and only. "Thanks, honey. That's sweet. But you know what, I have everything I need right here with you—and whether or not Dylan comes to his senses, that's up to him."

She sounded much more even and confident than she felt. Inside, she was a mess of unanswered questions and swirling emotion. But she had told Katie the truth. As upset as she was about Dylan's text, when it came down to it, Ariel had raised Katie from infancy on her own, ever since the divorce, and she had learned to be tough and make it when there was just the two of them.

But that didn't mean Dylan's rejection didn't hurt.

Ariel reached out and patted Katie's knee. "Enough about me. Tell me what I can do to help at school. Is this a I-need-to-vent-but-stay-out-of-it-mom moment, or is it jump-in-here-with-the-might-of-mom time?"

Katie rolled her eyes but snuggled under Ariel's outstretched arm. "You've talked to school before. It isn't getting better. Can't I homeschool? I know you work, but I'm fifteen. I can go online, and you can check it when you get home."

Ariel winced, looking back over the couch at the cardboard box that sat on the kitchen island. "About work ..."

Katie looked up at her. "What?"

"I got fired today," Ariel blurted before she could mull over in her mind the dozens of pros and cons of telling Katie now. But just like they always had been, she and Katie were a team. And Ariel didn't want to keep anything from her daughter.

Katie sat up, her dark eyes widening. "What? Work *and* Dylan? That sucks!"

Ariel nodded, her throat feeling thick. She started to rush into an explanation of how everything would be okay, how they had savings and she would get another job, and she would make sure that Katie was taken care of, but before she could deliver the platitudes, Katie held up a hand.

"Mom. You don't have to reassure me. I know we'll be all right. We always are. You always take care of things."

Ariel's throat burned and tightened even further. "Thanks, honey," she whispered.

Then, as if trying to lighten the suddenly heavy mood, Katie said, "Do you want a high school drama next, or a road trip movie?"

"You choose," Ariel said, picking up her phone and swiping to see that Dylan had sent another text. "Though I would guess that you aren't in the mood for any more high school drama."

The message on Ariel's phone shored up her resolve to completely ignore him for the remainder of the evening.

No reply? How childish.

She put her phone on silent and set it aside, his words burned into her retinas. *She* was childish? He was trying to break up over text!

Katie flopped back down onto the couch next to Ariel, and Ariel refocused on her daughter, snuggling her in close again. As the movie started, Ariel looked at Katie's profile. There was something troubled in her eyes. Ariel hugged her tighter.

Tomorrow, she would see what she could do to help Katie. And *then* she would confront Dylan.

***

In the fresh light of Saturday morning, Ariel sent off an email requesting to schedule a meeting with the principal of Crown Palms Academy and then showered and dressed. Katie came into the kitchen just as Ariel was making coffee, waving a text invite from her Art Club to a new gallery show that was going on later that day. With a hug and a promise to call if she wouldn't be home for dinner, Katie grabbed a muffin from the basket of them that Ariel had set on the counter and bounced off to get ready.

After Katie left, Ariel opened her laptop and dedicated the morning to surfing online for a few job openings and sending several emails to contacts putting out feelers. Then she spent a couple hours tidying up the house and decluttering—including dumping everything that had come from her office into the trash. She'd decided that she didn't want any of the bad juju that came along with the stapler or fancy company paperweight. And she didn't feel as though she was ready to face the little click-clackity metal ball desk doohickey that was supposed to bring her calm and Zen.

Everything sorted for the moment, and her afternoon unexpectedly clear, Ariel decided that a little retail therapy was in order—and when she studied herself in the hallway mirror, she added a salon trip and mani/pedi to her plans. A killer dress and a little pampering would bring her mood up. And it certainly wouldn't hurt to look her best when she dropped in on Dylan tonight. A cup of coffee and blueberry muffin along for the ride, Ariel grabbed her purse.

"On a mission," Ariel whispered as she let the front door close softly behind her.

Hours later, glow-up completed, Ariel drove toward Dylan's just as the Miami sun was setting over the tops of the palm trees, sinking low between the high-walled estates that dotted many of the residential areas in Coral Gables. It wasn't long before Ariel arrived at Dylan's place. The drive hadn't been overly long, but Ariel had been nervous the whole way. Her initial plan to drop in on Dylan unannounced had seemed bold and assertive at first, a way to declare that she wouldn't accept just a cookie-cutter text as the end of their relationship.

But as the freeway had stretched out in front of her, Miami proper giving way to the slightly less congested Gables, her confidence had begun to flag. Could she really just march up to his door and demand to know what had gone wrong? There had been no further messages from him after his second message, though she had refrained from sending her own replies asking if he was somehow joking (cruel, and unlike him, but a distant possibility), or if he had been taken hostage and was sending the message to signal her to alert the authorities (okay, so she'd seen it on social media—or maybe on a TV show—but Dylan was a high-powered, high-profile attorney, and didn't high-profile attorneys get kidnapped sometimes?).

Ariel slowed and turned her blinker on to ease into Dylan's neighborhood. Parking her Audi in the circular driveway, Ariel popped open her door and wiggled out, which was a feat in her red bodycon dress. Her hair was freshly blown out, and the dark tresses fell to her mid-back. Her heels clacked on the cobblestones as she carried a bottle of wine and a bouquet of red roses to the imposing front door.

There were lights on in the house, but she couldn't hear anything. And she knew that Dylan's housekeeper wasn't in on Saturdays, so they would be able to talk this out without anyone eavesdropping.

She didn't ring the doorbell, instead punching the access code she knew by heart into the number pad on the front door handle. Unlike her key card at the office, the access code worked, and she quietly slipped inside, gently nudging the door closed again with her hip as she cradled the wine and flowers.

Now inside, Ariel could hear Dylan's deep baritone coming from the kitchen area—or was it the dining room? She couldn't hear what he was saying, but she did hear him laugh. She followed the happy sound, her spirits buoyed, down the hall toward the kitchen.

When she emerged from the hallway, though, her spirits plummeted. Her mouth dropped open. And the bottle of wine slipped from her hand, crashing on the expensive slate tile.

"What is going on here?"

Dylan, who had been seated at the small dining set that occupied the eat-in portion of his vast kitchen, jumped up at the sound of her voice and the breaking glass. The young blonde seated across from him—who couldn't, in Ariel's estimation, be over the age of twenty-two—did not get up. The remains of a dinner were still on their plates. The fine china plates were a set that Ariel had bought for Mr. Ratface, Esquire, for Christmas just last year.

"Ari, what are you doing here?" Dylan's confused expression made Ariel laugh out loud, and his confusion quickly morphed into annoyance, judging by how his blue eyes clouded and narrowed and how his high forehead wrinkled.

"*This?*" Ariel waved the bouquet of roses at the blonde, who took a sip of her wine and calmly poured herself more as Ariel ranted. "*This* is why you broke up with me over text on my freaking birthday?"

The blonde uncrossed and crossed her legs, which seemed about a mile and a half longer than Ariel's. She remained silent but looked over at Dylan expectantly.

"I … I–That isn't any of your business. *I'm* not your business anymore. And how did you get in here, anyway?"

"The door code that I've used for the last *three years*, you jerk!" Ariel stomped her heel and caught a crunch of glass from the broken wine bottle. The acid smell of spilled wine wafted up to her. That must be what was causing her eyes to well—yes, that.

Dylan's posture stiffened, and he looked over at the blonde. "Mitzi, if you'll excuse us ..." Stepping away from the table, Dylan jogged over to Ariel and, grabbing her upper arm, spun her and marched her back down the hall.

"Let go of me," she hissed, shaking her arm free when they were halfway up the corridor. "I can't believe you! *Mitzi?* That's what you name a teacup Pomeranian, not a human being! Let me guess, all of your dates are long walks in the park?"

Dylan rolled his eyes at her, still herding her toward the foyer.

"Three years of my life, wasted. And it was, 'Ariel, you're the one,' and 'I can't believe how lucky I am to be with you.' What hogwash!"

Dylan didn't say anything until they were back at the front door and then he hissed low, "Look, I'm sorry your feelings are hurt." He paused then and reached up to rub the back of his neck. "You look *great* in that dress, wow."

"Spare me," she snapped, tossing back her long, dark hair, which was freshly layered and blown out—and yes, the dress was killer. All of which she hoped would make him seriously regret it when she walked out of here.

Dylan looked back down the hall, as if to verify they were still alone. "This isn't about love. That woman in there—Mitzi—is the daughter of one of the senior partners. This is purely … purely a—"

Ariel felt her blood run cold. "You dumped me so you could woo your way into making *partner?*"

At least he had the decency to look ashamed for a minute or two. "You know I've been trying for the last two years. Nothing has worked. I've got the highest percentage of settled real estate transactions in the firm, no run-ins with the bar, and my client accounts are all bringing in big cash to the firm. I needed a different tactic. And when you texted me that you'd been canned from your VP position …"

"You had to dump the dead weight. Got it." Ariel drew herself up to the tallest she could, which was five-six on a good day in two-inch heels. "Well, your loss, buddy. Don't come crawling back when Princess Cupcake in there decides being wifed up by a forty-something lawyer isn't quite as exciting as spending her daddy's money down in Coconut Grove and living single."

Dylan stepped back. "Get out," he said, his voice cold.

Ariel looked at him, taking in his neatly pressed chinos and light-blue polo. His dark, wavy hair was perfectly styled, and in any other instance, she would have found him absolutely irresistible standing in his boat shoes in the foyer of this lavish home. A place she had felt at home in the past few years.

But not now.

"Gladly," she retorted. She yanked the door open behind her and turned. Halfway out the door, she realized that she was still holding onto the roses. "Oh, and by the way—" she turned again, sharply, and tossed the roses at Dylan. The paper cone stuck to her sweaty palms, and Ariel watched as the paper ripped, and the flowers kept going, sending individual stems flinging at him like floral missiles. Ariel watched them each bounce off of him as he flailed to bat them away, protecting his face with one hand while he swatted with the other. Heaven forbid one of the thorns scratched his chiseled, always court-ready face "—Happy Birthday to me, you jerk."

She slammed the door behind her on her way to her car.

CHAPTER FOUR

When she arrived home, Ariel plopped down on the couch with a deep sigh, her glass of wine providing little solace from her heavy thoughts and her aching heart. There was no escaping that ugly vision of Dylan with his new flame—that plastic, generic, reality TV star, young girlfriend—and it left her with a feeling of crazy-stupid-betrayal that she just couldn't shake.

Curse Dylan—his handsome face and his charming smile! What a fraud he had turned out to be! The tears threatened to come. She raised her glass of wine in toast to her own foolishness. How could she have ever trusted him? She stared at the mantel, at the pictures they'd taken together in happier times—before Dylan had gone and broken all his promises. Ariel stood from the couch, grabbed a framed photo from the mantel of her and Dylan together, and hurled it into the fireplace.

Ariel glanced around her living room for more photos to relegate to the flames. On top of a nearby bookcase, she saw a stack of photo albums. Curious, she set her wine down and retrieved them—she hadn't taken a photo on film in years, and she'd forgotten what these old albums even contained.

She carefully set the stack on the table in front of the couch and sat down to go through them. "Endless Harbor" was etched across the top volume's leather cover, sending a wave of nostalgia over Ariel as she picked it up, returning to the couch to open the album's fragile pages.

Inside was a collection of memories from her childhood summers in Maine. There was her father and her sister, before he'd left them—life before the heartbreak and loss. The old, Victorian house with its wraparound porch and gorgeous grounds, acres filled with beautiful gardens and views of the lonely ocean. It all came back to life in her mind—the place her father, and she, had loved most in the world: Endless Harbor.

Ariel closed her eyes as tears flowed down her cheeks, remembering summers spent there in all its beauty. The walk-in fireplace in the living room. The giant, antique grandfather clock in the entryway. The beautiful, hand-carved banister leading up to the second floor. The quaint, little, winding roads that lead to the house perched on the bluffs.

She thought about the quiet, little marina where they would rent out boat after boat after boat. All day long. She recalled the time she had fallen overboard and had to be rescued. Her father had thrown her a lifesaver and told her to grab onto it and stay afloat until he could get to her. Then he had been beside her, swimming strongly to shore, towing her in.

Ariel felt a flashback of falling into the water that day, of the cold, and of the fear. And then she experienced all over the relief and joy she had felt, knowing that her father was coming to rescue her. Those had been the good times. Too bad there was no way he was coming to rescue her now.

The summer that she was fifteen, her father had gone missing.

The police had come, and they'd taken the missing persons report— no signs of foul play, they'd said—and there had been no sign of Lee Briggs ever since. They had gone through the arduous process of having him declared legally deceased when Ariel's mother had passed away, since his name had still been on the house deed. Probate had been a bear.

But Ariel had always held out hope, even when she'd been sweating in a kitchen in Paris, that she would catch a glimpse of her father somewhere—a moment, a chance meeting, and he would explain everything. That he was still out there, and he would make it make sense.

Ariel thumbed through the album slowly, feeling the weight of her youth like a heavy stone in her heart. Memories tumbled out of the crackly, old pages, the noise reminiscent of rain that would pound the roof of the Endless Harbor house, with its Victorian grandeur and wraparound porch. The beautiful, lonely ocean that had crashed the rocky cliffs that edged the property had been so special to her and her father alike. He'd always wanted to turn it into something more, but life had had other plans.

The smile on Ariel's tired face faltered as she let all those lovely memories wash over her until nothing was left but a twinge of sadness for all that had been lost. Lost, just like her job and her chance at love. At least this time, it was her first time being fired. As for love, she knew all too well the feeling of being disappointed and having to muster the courage to start all over. A youthful romance and quickie marriage to Katie's father had been enough to make her gun-shy for years. And Dylan hadn't helped.

15

She took a long drink of wine and sat there in her sadness, grateful at least that Katie was asleep and not here to see her mother having a breakdown. Ariel had never felt that she was all that strong—no, it had been her sister, Charlene, who had always been the tough one.

Ariel thought about how her sister had always been so strong—when Lee Briggs had disappeared, when their mom had died, when Ariel had gone through her divorce. No matter what sadness or tragedy befell them, Charlene was strong, like a mighty oak that stood tall against the raging storm.

And then, as Ariel came to the last page of the album—a photo of her father standing on the cliffs at Endless Harbor—Ariel recalled the last conversation she'd had with her dad. His voice had trembled as they'd walked along the beach together, dusk bleeding into twilight.

"Dad, do you really think you can do it?" she asked.

"I'm certain of it," he said, his face bright with the dream of turning their house into an inn. "I'm sure there'll be plenty of people who will want to stay here."

A spark of hope flared inside her. The photos of Maine made her ache for a life away from Miami. Up there, the sky stretched on forever, and the kind people said hello to strangers on the street. That world was so distant from the one she experienced here, where the streets smelled of exhaust, and people forgot how to be polite. There would be no snotty suburbanite bullies to plague Katie. And the house was still there.

She put the photo album down and sighed. Maybe it was time for a change. Could she uproot their life and move to Maine, to Leeside? It was sitting empty, after all. Charlene wasn't doing anything but letting it sit. And Katie was miserable in school—maybe in Maine, Ariel *could* homeschool her. Ariel daydreamed of low-hanging chandeliers and wallpaper striped with soft colors. Maybe she could bring joy back into her home once more.

She imagined walking through the dusty rooms, throwing open the windows to let in fresh air and light, clearing out the cobwebs, and making it a place that could be loved again; a place where people could come and stay, where memories could be made and shared. She sighed as she closed the lid of the old photo album. Maybe the crazy idea wasn't so crazy after all.

One more glass of wine and then she would think about it— seriously. As she sipped, Ariel couldn't resist sifting back through the photos. The idea of turning the house into a Bed and Breakfast was now taking shape in her imagination. It would be hard work—she'd have to redecorate, replace the furniture and kitchen, maybe even replace structural elements of the house itself.

But the thought of running her own inn and starting a new life sparked wonders within her. Tourists taking pictures, fishing on chartered boats, and dancing in the front yard under fairy lights, dining al fresco to the sound of the sea—the images brought a smile to her face. Ariel pictured them getting lost in the local town, buying souvenirs, and chatting with old townspeople. There was a growing excitement that swirled in and nudged aside the bad feelings brought on by her breakup—at least a little. A thrill of possibility replaced the fear.

Ariel knew it was time to call her sister.

CHAPTER FIVE

"I have an idea," Ariel said, the words coming out in a rush. "Don't hang up."

She heard Charlene sigh on the other end. The two of them had lived apart for years, but no distance or time could dull the tight bond and familiarity between them. As she spoke—and her sister seemed to gird herself to counter whatever Ariel was about to propose—Ariel felt the warmth and love that came across even in her sister's exasperated breath.

"Well, hello to you, too, stranger," Charlene said. "What is it now?"

"Don't act like you don't have your own wild ideas every five minutes," Ariel said, picturing her sister in the big, open kitchen of her coastal two-story, sipping tea and catching up on celebrity gossip magazines. Charlene's kids would be asleep by now, and maybe even Kurt would be dozing too. Charlie had always been a night owl, the opposite of her early-to-rise, construction-foreman husband. "How many months did I stay on that skincare subscription scam you were peddling last year?"

"Pffft." Charlene scoffed, and Ariel could hear the pages flipping in whatever tabloid she was reading. "Your skin looks amazing. You can't deny that."

"Nor can I deny all of the recruitment calls I *still* get because you gave that company my cell phone number. And my skin looks amazing because of the fine salt air of Miami and the fact that I am younger than you are."

"Two whole years! And there's sea air in Maine a'plenty. Besides, we're not talking about me, hun. We're talking about you and whatever this grand idea is that has caused this late-night call."

"We're in the same time zone, Charlie. It's only nine o'clock."

"Out with it!" Charlene said, sounding half exasperated and half amused. "I'm getting to the juicy parts of *A-List Tattler*, and you seem to be stalling."

Ariel's heart began to race with panic. She knew her sister would not be thrilled about the idea, and the thought of facing her disapproval filled Ariel with dread. Of course, Charlie had her own disastrous business sense, but Ariel herself was supposed to be the one who had already made it. If she told her sister that she'd lost it all and wanted to come crawling back home, Ariel was sure that Charlie would see it as a failure. It wouldn't be said out loud, but Ariel would *feel* it. Besides that, Charlie had an emotional reason for letting Leeside go to rot. Deep down, Ariel sensed that her sister wanted all of the bad memories there to disintegrate with the house itself.

Ariel took a deep breath, trying to steady her nerves.

"Our old house," Ariel worked up the courage to say. Rushing, she pushed out, "Dad's old house. I want to turn it into an inn. Well, a B&B. I want to leave Miami and come home to Maine. To start life all over. I know it's going to be a lot of work, but I think it's worth it. The place has so much potential, and I know that with some effort and money, we can turn it into something special. I can cook there. I can make it work." She took a breath and paused. "What do you think?"

Charlene's voice dripped with incredulity. "You think *we* can renovate the entire house? It's been sitting empty for years, and the amount of work that needs to be done is staggering. We don't have the money or the experience to take on something like this."

"You're married to a man who lives and breathes construction."

"And who will surely see this as another one of my—how did you put it—*wild ideas*?"

Ariel sighed. "I know it's not going to be easy, but I think we can make it happen. We might have to get loans, but we'll be able to run the house as a business and turn a profit. One that doesn't involve any kind of catalog or recruitment."

Charlene snorted over the line, and Ariel sensed she was toeing a fine line. Charlene, for all her many pluses, had never quite found what she wanted to do with her life. She had a beautiful home and a marriage that had lasted, but Ariel wondered if her sister's many forays into hinky, get-rich-quick companies were a reach for something outside of her suburban, coastal life. "Plus, it's not just about the money, it's about preserving our family home."

"Preserving it? Ariel, the house is falling apart. It would be more practical to just tear it down and start fresh. And even if we did have the money, or got loans, where are we going to find the time to work on the renovation? We both have our own lives and responsibilities. Ari, I think you're drunk," Charlene said, her voice heavy with concern. The page flipping had stopped.

"I'm not. Maybe tipsy. But even so, I'm thinking more clearly than I have in *years*."

"You're still not making any sense. Where is this coming from? You have a life in Miami—a good job. And Dylan. And Katie has school, and her friends."

Ariel let her tears well anew. "Oh, Charlie," she sobbed, finally breaking. "I don't have any of those things. Jim Chambers took over Opulent, and I got fired. And Dylan *dumped* me. And Katie … Katie is having the worst time in school. These bullies …"

She broke off into a series of gut-deep sobs that her sister stayed silent through. After she had managed to regain her breath and half her composure, Ariel finished, "Things are awful. I just want to be back where I knew I was happy, once." She sniffled deeply, watery eyes wandering the living room for the box of tissues she knew was nearby.

"Ariel, you haven't seen that house in twenty years," Charlene said gently but firmly. "It's a disaster. If you want to come for a visit, sure. I will make up the guest room, and you and Katie can come and stay in pajamas for a week and skip schoolwork and life and just eat ice cream and watch TV. But the house, yeesh. When Dad … uhm … when he left—"

"*Disappeared*," Ariel said forcefully. "Abandoned his family."

"We don't know that," Charlene said, her voice taking on the softness of a hostage negotiator. "But that's a whole other talk for a different night. When he left, that left mom to keep up everything, which she was not great at."

"And when she died? Why didn't you do anything with Leeside?"

"I didn't have the time to look after the house. It's a time capsule, Ari. A dusty, termite-ridden, moldy time capsule. I have the kids."

"But you didn't sell it."

Charlie sighed heavily. "Fine! It's complicated. Is that what you're getting at? Yes, it is."

Having located the tissues, Ariel blew her nose loudly. "I just feel like it's time for a change. The house is sitting there. It's just sitting there, empty like my heart right now. I should do something with it. I feel like I should start a *new* life. And if I can tear that thing down and build up something beautiful out of it, then maybe I can do the same with the absolute wreck that my life is right now. Do you get it?"

"Yes," her sister said, "but—"

Ariel interrupted, her voice desperate even to her own ears. "Don't you ever feel, Charlie, like you've been stuck in one place for *far* too long, and, like, you're just *desperate* for something new?"

Ariel stopped pacing—she hadn't really realized that she'd been doing it until she found herself in the kitchen—and sat down at her own kitchen counter, staring out the window at the darkened street, the looming silhouettes of the palm trees that lined her street looking like giants in the moonlight. She ran her fingers across her squeaky-clean kitchen island, the marble cool under her fingers. She could almost feel the heat from the kitchens she'd worked at in France, the constant chatter of her staff, the pressure of creating new and exciting dishes. She rarely cooked now. How long had it been since she'd actually created something unique? Her time with Opulent had certainly put her hands-on culinary skills on the back burner.

Ariel knew, deep down, that her true passion was in cooking and providing a place where people could relax and enjoy their time, taking a break from their busy lives. That had been the surface goal of Opulent Ice—but that had seemed to quickly crumble under corporate greed. The idea of running a bed and breakfast in Maine, where she could reconnect with nature, cook, and most importantly, create a safe and nurturing environment for her daughter, felt like the perfect escape from the fast-paced city. Katie would do much better in a small town where the community was tight-knit, and people looked out for each other.

And she hadn't realized how much Katie's school problems had been weighing on her mind. Now, with her firing from Opulent and Dylan's unexpected exit, Ariel could find a place for herself and Katie where they could both thrive again. Ariel yearned for something simpler, something more relaxed, and most importantly, a safer place for her daughter.

Charlene wasn't saying anything. Ariel closed her eyes and let her mind drift to the small, coastal town of Endless Harbor, Maine. She imagined the crisp, salty air and the sound of the waves crashing against the shore. She pictured a charming bed and breakfast nestled among the rocky cliffs, where she could cook gourmet breakfasts for her guests, using the freshest local ingredients and creating unique and delicious recipes. She could see herself waking up early in the morning to prepare breakfast for her guests and spending the rest of the day exploring the town and getting reacquainted with the locals.

The silence remained unbroken a few more beats, and Charlene's reply sounded almost tearful as she said gently, "Ariel, you really are crazy, but it's a beautiful idea."

Ariel whispered, "You mean—"

"Pack up, I guess," Charlie said with a sigh. "I can't promise I'll be any help, or that Kurt will be either, but I can't fault you for wanting a fresh start. I'll get the paperwork started with Holcomb in the morning to get the deed transferred over to you."

Holcomb! Ariel remembered the voicemail.

"Oh, you know he called me, Holcomb. I think he meant to call you. Can you ask him when you talk to him what it was that he wanted?"

"Yes. Now, goodnight. Get some sleep. And if you need me to come to Miami and sock anyone in the nose for you—job or ex-boyfriend—you let me know."

"No nose-socking," Ariel said, suddenly realizing how exhausted she was. "I'll be in Maine with you soon, Char. And I will take you up on that ice cream and pajama offer."

"Get here fast," Charlene warned. "Ice cream doesn't last long in this house."

With a heartfelt exchange of "I love yous," the call ended, and Ariel was left again in her quiet house with her new future now said out loud, spoken into the universe.

That meant she had to jump into it—and that she had to break the news to Katie.

CHAPTER SIX

Even though Ariel knew that a completely new life awaited, the finality of the trunk slamming sounded *too* final.

She had been focused for days on fighting the nervousness and slight nausea that had plagued her as she'd packed up her Miami house and prepared for the transition to Maine. Pulled in too many directions for any real rest, she resorted to letting Katie skip the last day of school for the week, and they'd spent their last Friday as Floridians cleaning out guest rooms full of furniture and expensive curtains and tchotchkes that had never been seen by any guests.

As she'd packed away an adorable trio of delicate porcelain dolls that had been perched on a bookshelf in one of the rooms, Ariel reflected on how so much of her life in Miami had been just like these rooms—pretty, well-arranged when you looked from the outside, but empty. There would be new places for these things once they got to Endless Harbor, and rooms that would be filled with people who enjoyed them. Maybe a few new things in Ariel's life that would make her feel fulfilled too.

Still, as Ariel climbed into the driver's seat of her SUV, she felt the weighty pull of what she had lost. This was the house where she and her ex-husband had first settled, where Katie had been brought home from the hospital after she'd been born, and where the good memories outweighed the bad—even the divorce and being dumped by Dylan. Here, they'd had dinner get-togethers and birthday parties, fireworks being set off all over the neighborhood for the fourth of July, the balmy nights in winter, and the epic summer thunderstorms.

As Ariel gave one last look up the driveway to the beach-white Spanish bungalow that they had called home, she said a silent goodbye to the warmth and familiarity of Miami for the long drive up to Maine. Then she climbed into the driver's seat and craned over the seat to look at Katie.

Ariel could tell that Katie was not happy about the move, despite her assurances that it would be good for them both. All morning, Katie had been sullen and short in her responses.

"Ready to go?" Ariel tried to put some cheer into her voice.

Katie just stared out the window, watching the house as Ariel put the SUV in reverse and drove away for the last time.

The drive was a long and scenic journey. As they left the bustling city of Miami and headed north on the Florida Turnpike, urban congestion gave way to the flat, sprawling landscape of southern Florida, with its vast fields of sugarcane and its cookie-cutter, suburban neighborhoods.

Ariel piloted the SUV north, passing through the Florida panhandle and into the rolling hills and dense forests of Georgia. Along the way, she oooh'd and ahhhh'd over the small towns and charming rural communities that sprung up on either side of the freeway. But Katie still would not be swayed from her sulking. In fact, she barely said a word even on their pit stops, preferring to keep her earbuds in and the music on her phone cranked up so loud that Ariel could hear it, despite the headphones.

They stopped for the night in Savannah, Georgia. After burgers and fries at an all-night diner, they each climbed into separate twin beds in a generic room at a quick-stop hotel just off the freeway feeder road. Ariel was too exhausted to try to coax a conversation out of Katie. And despite her exhaustion, Ariel lay awake even after Katie was softly snoring. She stared at the rotating ceiling fan, her mind whirling. She had been so focused on making this plan work that she hadn't stopped to consider how difficult it might be for her daughter.

"I love you, Katie," Ariel whispered across the dark of the hotel room.

There was no reply, which Ariel had expected.

Her eyes pricking with tears, Ariel tried to drift off, hoping to dream pleasant dreams of a happy future, despite the turmoil swirling through her wide-awake mind.

***

The next morning, they got an earlier start after donuts and coffee in the hotel lobby. Katie seemed in somewhat better spirits. She sat up front with Ariel instead of in the back of the car, which was a small win.

Ariel could see the anticipation building in Katie's face as they got underway for the day. She could sense that her daughter's mood was starting to lift as they got farther and farther from Miami. Katie wasn't exactly chatty, but they didn't ride in awkward silence as they had the day before.

After their first snack stop, Katie turned to Ariel as soon as they exited back to the main concourse toward Virginia.

"Mom, what's the high school in Endless Harbor like? Is it really different from my school in Miami?"

Ariel looked sideways at her daughter. *Ah, the real issue comes out.* "It's definitely different, honey. Endless Harbor is a small town, so the school is smaller than what you're used to. But that's not necessarily a bad thing. The teachers know the students well, and they're more invested in their success. I thought you wanted to homeschool?"

"Maybe. I'm still thinking about it. But what about the classes? Will they be as good as they were in Miami?"

"Well, if you're talking about EHHS, there's a great academic program, and you'll have a lot more opportunities to get involved in extracurricular activities and clubs now that I'll be home more. I was on the debate team and the school newspaper when I was in high school there. Maybe you could start that Adventure Quest club you always talked about but—"

"Brittney Tanner made fun of me and threw all my flyers for the club into the boy's bathroom? Yeah. I bet there's a Brittney in this school. Every school has a Brittney. There's no escaping her."

Ariel didn't reply right away, waiting.

"Maybe I will homeschool," Katie said, her lips twisting.

As she drove, Ariel's thoughts drifted back to her high school days at Endless Harbor High. She remembered the excitement of starting high school, the new faces, and the sense of endless possibility. Her first day had been nerve-wracking, but she had quickly found her place among a group of friends who were as artsy as she was—while Ariel had loved cooking from a young age, her group had been drama kids, band geeks, and friends who drew and painted. Though a small town, the wild coast of Endless Harbor had seemed to inspire many a person. Ariel and her friends had spent countless hours working on projects and studying for exams, and Ariel was grateful to have had them by her side.

But not all her memories of school were positive. She also remembered the constant pressure to fit in, the fear of not being accepted, and the relentless, small-town gossip that seemed to spread like wildfire. She'd been mocked for spending time in her garden instead of at beach get-togethers and parties and for her elaborate lunches. She was taunted when her father had disappeared. She would never forget how it made her feel small and insignificant. It was moments like these that made her dread going to school each day. If it hadn't been for Charlene being there for her, even after she'd graduated ahead of Ariel, Ariel wasn't sure she would have stuck it out until her own senior year.

Despite the challenges, Ariel persevered and found solace in her creative outlet—cooking. She spent countless hours in the kitchen of Leeside, pouring her heart and soul into each dish and technique, even before she'd been able to go off to culinary school. It was there that'd she found a sense of peace and a place where she could be herself without fear of judgment.

High school had been a rollercoaster ride of emotions, but it had also shaped her into the person she was today. She had learned the importance of resilience, self-love, and the value of real friendship. And even though she wouldn't want to go back to those days, she was grateful for the memories that had made her who she was.

Ariel tried to choose her words carefully. "People are different everywhere you go. You'll make friends in no time. And you never know, you might find that you like it there *better* than Miami."

Katie looked out the window again, a sign that she was slipping away once more. "I hope so, but I'm worried."

Ariel's heart warmed at the confession—in the teen years, she would take any small win she could get, and Katie admitting to being scared at least showed that Katie still trusted her. Ariel's chest tightened when she thought of how much was in front of them—she was worried too. She was still getting past the sting of two major life losses, and she didn't want Katie to feel she had to bear the burden or fallout from either.

"I understand, sweetie. It's normal to feel that way. But you're smart, strong, confident, and kind. You'll make friends and find your place here. I'm here for you, and we'll get through this together." She reached over and squeezed Katie's hand.

Katie squeezed back and actually smiled.

"Are you looking forward to seeing the house?" Ariel asked, training her eyes back on the road ahead.

They had reached the border of Virginia, and the landscape had begun to change again. The forests were giving way to rolling hills and winding rivers, and Ariel could start to see the first signs of previous snow.

Katie noticed it too—small islands of white in otherwise cold, muddy stretches of land. But she perked up. "Is that snow?"

"It is," Ariel said, bemused.

"Awesome! You know, I am, Mom. I think I *am* looking forward to seeing the house." Katie was studying the landscape outside with wide, awed eyes.

"To our new adventure together, then," Ariel said.

"Together," Katie agreed. Then, with a sheepish look over at her mother, she popped her earbuds in and began fiddling again with her phone. They had made it a couple hours down the road without Katie resorting to her phone, so Ariel chalked that up in the win column as well.

Ariel checked the clock on the SUV—if they drove for about four hours, they could make their stop in Endless Harbor by dinnertime. Just as she was looking back to the road ahead, her phone dinged with a missed call, and her screen said she had a voicemail. She frowned. She'd thought that she'd put her phone on completely silent for the drive.

She said the voice command that would wake the phone up and then asked her message to be played. The voice of the family lawyer— Holcomb—came over the car speakers.

"Hey, Ariel. I just got all the paperwork to your sister for your dad's old place. I told her about a business proposition that fell into my lap a couple weeks ago. Talk it over when you get to Maine and then please give me a call."

A business proposition? That could be interesting. She would call him as soon as they arrived in Maine.

As they pressed toward their new home, Ariel felt a sense of warmth, a feeling of closeness, and a renewed glimmer of hope for the mother-daughter bond between herself and Katie. And now, the added excitement   of   *possibility.*

CHAPTER SEVEN

As Ariel and Katie entered the last leg of their trip, easing into the northeastern states, the landscape became increasingly rugged and wild. They passed through the towering peaks of the Appalachian Mountains and the dense forests of the Adirondacks. The weather was starting to get colder, and the snow seemed ready to fall from the ominous, gray skies.

As they crossed the border of Maine, the landscape changed again, becoming more rocky and rugged. On both sides of the freeway were dense forests giving glimpses through their trunks at beaches along the rocky coastline, with the Atlantic Ocean on one side and pine forests on the other. And as they drove into the quaint town of Endless Harbor, they were surrounded by the sea and the sound of seagulls. It would have all been quite summery, if not for the fact that it had recently snowed.

The road to the new-old house was winding and narrow, and the houses along the way—a collection of millionaires' mansions tucked by the cliffs—rubbed shoulders (and back yards) with small, quaint, coastal bungalows. The latter were small and colorful, with plenty of lobster shacks and seafood restaurants interspersed to keep anyone happy. The sea air was fresh and invigorating, and the views of the ocean were breathtaking. But Ariel tried her best to not get distracted, carefully navigating the ice-crunchy roadway.

Katie was not paying attention to the charm. When they arrived in Endless Harbor, the first thing that Katie said was, "Mom, it's *cold* here."

It was true—it was bitter cold. It was a stark contrast to the warm and sunny climate she was used to in Miami. The snow was waist-high in drifts along the sides of the road, and the frigid winds would cut through their clothing. Ariel could imagine her fingers and toes going numb in minutes if she were out in the weather, and she cranked up the car heater gratefully. She knew that she would never get used to this kind of cold again. How had she managed it as a kid?

The gravel of the cleared driveway crunched under her SUV tires as Ariel finally pulled up to her father's old Victorian.

"This is it," Ariel said, looking at the house with a mix of excitement and trepidation. "This is our future."

As they finally turned down the long driveway that led to the house, Ariel could feel her own excitement building. She had a vision for what this house could be, and she was determined to make it a reality, no matter how difficult the road ahead might be.

When they stopped, Ariel looked at the house through the front windshield, and a smile spread across her face. "I remember so many good times at this place," she said. "It's not as bad as Charlie made it out to be—we can make this work!"

Katie looked at the house. Her face scrunched. Ariel knew she was only focusing on the bad. Sure, ice and snow covered the roof and the windows, the paint was peeling, the porch was sagging, and the chimneys looked like they were about to collapse, but you had to look past that to the potential.

"Mom," Katie said, her voice trembling, "on second thought, I don't think I can do this. I want to go back to Miami. I'll be homeschooled there instead of us having to move. That will take care of Brittney and her bots. Please. *Please*?"

Ariel made sure the car was in park and turned to her daughter. "I know it's tough, Katie. But we're here now, and we have to make the best of it. Let's go inside and see what we can do with it."

As they walked inside the house, even Ariel couldn't shake the feeling of dread that had settled deep in her chest. The house was cold, damp, and dark, with ice on the windows and water damage everywhere. The floors were creaky, and several of the interior walls were cracked. And with no heating turned on, Katie could see her breath in the air. It was hard to imagine how they would ever turn this place into a home, let alone a B&B. In fact, Ariel was a little uncertain of where they would sleep for the night.

"I guess there was no cleaning service before we got here," Katie mumbled.

Enough was enough. Ariel was tired, Katie was likely tired, but Katie's attitude was hurting her feelings. Ariel decided to be direct. "Look. I know you're not excited about this move, Katie. I want you to know that I understand. I know this is a big change, and it can be scary. But I promise you, *it's going to be okay*. You'll make new friends, you'll have a new start, and hopefully, you will have a better school experience. But none of that can happen right now, ten minutes after we arrive. And no, there was no cleaning service who would come up here and tackle this place for anything less than a thousand dollars *to start*, which is not a wise expenditure when we have our own two—four—hands. "

Ariel broke off, her breath puffing faster into the cold.

Katie's face softened a little, and she turned to her mother. "I know you're trying to do what's best for us, Mom. I'll *try* to make the best of it."

Ariel pulled Katie into a hug. "That's all I can ask for, sweetie. I promise you that we'll make this work."

Ariel and Katie further explored the house, and they were met with a sight that was nothing short of overwhelming. The once-beautiful home was now a shell of its former self, with peeling wallpaper, water-damaged floors, and a musty smell that hung heavy in the air.

Ariel stopped in the middle of the kitchen, which she remembered as being so grand and beautiful—the place she'd discovered so much. Her heart sank as she took in the state of disrepair. The once-beautiful room was now a shadow of its former self. Tears rose at the sight before her.

Ariel walked slowly around the kitchen, taking in each detail. The shelves were dusty, the countertops were chipped, and the cabinets were covered in grime. It was clear that the kitchen had been neglected for years. As she continued to look around, Ariel began to picture what the kitchen looked like in its prime. She imagined the wide, smooth countertops, the gleaming, copper pots and pans hanging from the ceiling, and the beautiful, mosaic tiles adorning the walls. The room had once been the heart of the home, a place where meals were cooked, and memories were made.

The contrast between the past and present was stark, and Ariel was sad for the state of the once-beautiful place. How in the world could she bring it back? It seemed insurmountable.

Katie stopped beside Ariel, wrapping her arms around her mother's shoulders. "It's okay, Mom," she said. "We'll figure it out together. Like you said, we'll make it work."

Ariel felt a wave of relief wash over her as she hugged her daughter back. She had been so afraid of how Katie would react to seeing what Ariel saw, but her daughter's understanding and support was more than she could have hoped for.

"Thank you, Katie," Ariel said, her voice choked with emotion. "Charlie said it was bad, but I wasn't expecting this. I promise, I'll make it right."

"It's okay, Mom," Katie said, giving her mother a reassuring squeeze. "You tell me not to close off, so don't you. We're a team. Now, how do we get the heat on?"

As they sat together at the rickety kitchen table that was still in the open dining room, hope and determination welled up inside of Ariel. She pulled out a blueprint of the house that Charlie had sent so that Ariel could start planning.

Katie propped her chin in one hand and looked at Ariel. "You think the boiler's in the basement?"

"Let's see, chickdee," she said and then winced internally. The nickname—chickadee—had been one that Dylan had used with Katie, and it had become second nature for Ariel to pick up the moniker. But the last thing she wanted right now was to be sitting in these dismal circumstances, thinking about Dylan. But it was too late, she guessed.

Ariel's heart ached as she thought about Dylan. He had been her rock for the last three years, and she had foolishly believed that he would be there for her and Katie when they needed him most. But he hadn't, and he wouldn't now.

In fact, Ariel had called him to come pick up a few boxes of his stuff that she'd collected as she'd packed to move, but he had never answered. She'd donated them to the local thrift store. The house seemed even more depressing and run-down after her thoughts wandered to Dylan. The furniture was covered with sheets, the floorboards were creaking underfoot, and cobwebs were covering every corner. The wallpaper was yellowed with age, and the paint on the walls was chipped and peeling. The kitchen was outdated for sure, but it seemed like the appliances were from another era—Ariel was sure they had not been replaced since her mother had died. The bedrooms upstairs were moldy, and the mattresses had been exposed to the elements for so long that they were growing all manner of flora. Ariel winced when she remembered Charlene warning her about this very thing. The seasons had taken their toll on the house.

As she looked around the dilapidated dining room, Ariel knew that it would be a long and difficult road to bring the house back to life.

Katie tapped the open blueprint in front of Ariel, bringing her back to the present.

"Mom, the boiler?"

Ariel's eyes scanned until she found where the main heating unit resided. She grinned and tried to look positive when she stood from the table.

"Got it! How about we get some heat on?"

CHAPTER EIGHT

"I know absolutely nothing about boilers," Ariel said, her breath making clouds in the frigid air of the basement. Katie held a flashlight aloft, the only source of light they had down here since all of the hanging bulbs had long since burned out. Ariel and Katie were huddled together, trying to keep warm as they worked on the boiler. Ariel had been trying to get it to turn on for the past hour, but to no avail. Katie's phone was nearly out of battery from playing DIY boiler repair videos from online, and she was getting increasingly frustrated. Ariel was starting to lose patience as well.

"This is ridiculous, Mom," Katie said, her teeth chattering. "Why can't we just call a repairman? Or Aunt Charlie? Can't Uncle Kurt fix this kind of stuff? We could go to a hotel for the night."

"Because it's too late in the day to call anyone out," Ariel replied, her voice tinged with frustration. "And Aunt Charlie would just say I told you so. It took a lot of convincing for me to get her onboard with the whole bed and breakfast idea. We're going to have to figure this out ourselves."

The hotel did sound like a good idea, but would that be admitting defeat? Ariel thought that if they couldn't get some kind of heat on in the house for the night, then that might be where they ultimately ended up.

There were no results when she fiddled with the boiler's controls for the hundred and sixtieth time, but as she crouched on the damp concrete floor, she heard a strange rustling sound coming from the far corner of the basement. "What is that?" she muttered to herself.

"I don't know, but it's creeping me out," Katie said, her eyes wide with fear.

Ariel stood and grabbed the flashlight from Katie. She cautiously made her way over to the corner of the basement, with Katie following close behind. They were confronted with a labyrinthian maze that seemed to stretch out in every direction.

As Ariel made her way through the cluttered basement, she pushed down a sense of unease. The musty smell of damp earth and mold seemed to cling to the air, and it was hard to navigate through the boxes and old furniture that seemed to stretch out in every direction. As they reached a stack of boxes that was blocking them from seeing the farthest part of the basement, the same strange rustling sound caught their attention again.

"What *was* that?" Katie asked, her voice trembling with fear. Ariel's heart began to race as she cautiously peered around the stack of boxes.

"Honey, I—"

Suddenly, a large raccoon jumped out from the corner of the room. The animal's fur was matted and dirty, and its eyes gleamed with a wild and feral intelligence. It let out a loud screech, baring its sharp teeth as it lunged at them.

Ariel and Katie both let out screams of their own and ran back up the stairs as fast as they could. Ariel pushed Katie in front of her, motherly instinct making her move almost reflexively.

"Go, go, go, go!" she hollered, the sound of small, scrabbling claws on the rickety stairs behind them driving her to new heights of terror. Katie tumbled through the basement door and into the kitchen, Ariel hot on her heels.

They slammed the basement door shut behind them. There was a meaty *thud* against the other side of the door that caused both of them to shriek again. Ariel's heart was pounding with adrenaline as they leaned against the door, each trying to catch their breath.

"That was too close," Katie said, her voice shaking. "I thought it was going to kill us. Or at least seriously transmit some mutant form of rabies."

"Me too," Ariel replied, still trying to steady her racing heart. "We'll have to call an exterminator to take care of it. There is definitely no YouTube video that I would follow to DIY getting rid of that monster."

"Why hasn't it frozen to death? It's *so cold* in here."

As she tried to shake off the fear and shock, Ariel shook her head. "I have no idea. Maybe it is a mutant."

Ariel was grateful to be out of the basement, but she was also worried about the state of the house. The raccoon may have caused damage and nested in the insulation, electrical, or other important places. So, the battle was against the house and the mutant invaders? Double pressure.

"Did I mention that was close?" Ariel said, her heart still pounding in her chest.

"Too close," Katie parroted, looking as though she was still in shock.

"Well, I think it's safe to say we're not going to be getting the heat on tonight," Ariel said.

Beside her, Katie groaned. "Worst. Move. Ever."

***

Ariel and Katie were sitting on the couch, still trying to shake off the surprise of the raccoon incident in the basement. That distinctive, musty smell of damp earth and mold seemed to linger in Ariel's nostrils, the memory of the animal's screech and bared teeth still fresh in her mind.

"No hotels with vacancies for the night," Ariel said dejectedly after she'd hung up on her third call. "At least we know that Endless Harbor needs another place for people to stay."

Katie, who was under a comedically large stack of blankets that they had brought in from the car, whined. "Not helpful."

"I'm going to try and find a pizza place that delivers," Ariel said, pulling out her phone. She scrolled through a quick restaurant search, looking for a nearby restaurant that would deliver to their remote location. Pizza wasn't the most gourmet thing, but Ariel would have her five-star kitchen and fancy dinner plans soon enough. Tonight, all she wanted was some warmth and something to feed both of them. They'd have to figure out where in the house to crash for the night, and soon—Ariel peeked out a window in the kitchen to see that the sunlight was beginning to wane.

"Sounds good," Katie replied, still looking a little pale. She hugged her knees to her chest, her eyes fixed on the door as if she expected the raccoon to come bursting through at any moment.

A few minutes after Ariel had stood to pace the house, trying to get phone reception, there was a knock on the door.

"I'll get it," Ariel said, getting up from the couch. She walked to the door hesitantly, her hand shaking as she reached for the knob. She silently chided herself. What could be out there, a knocking racoon?

She opened the door to find an old woman standing on the porch.

"Hello there, I'm Doris, a friend of your parents," the woman said, her voice rough and raspy.

The woman had wild, unkempt hair that was a mix of gray and white, and her eyes were a piercing blue. She was short, only about five-foot-nothing, and her face was lined with wrinkles and crevices that seemed to tell the story of a life full of laughter, tears, and a lot of sun exposure.

As Ariel looked at Doris, she was instantly struck by the woman's eccentric and colorful winter outfit. It was a mix of fur, wool, and corduroy in various shades of browns and greens. The centerpiece of the outfit was a vintage fur coat, possibly fox or raccoon—Ariel should ask if Doris was a trapper of some sort—that seemed to be at least two sizes too big for her. The coat had a large, shaggy collar and cuffs that were adorned with large, ornate brooches.

Underneath the coat, Doris wore a patchwork, corduroy dress that had mismatched buttons running down the front and a large, asymmetrical hemline that ended just above her knee-high, fur-lined boots. The boots were made of a dark brown leather and capped with brass buckles.

She'd completed the outfit with a pair of thick, woolen tights in a bright orange color, and a pair of fingerless gloves made of a soft, knitted yarn. The gloves were circled with colorful pom-poms on the cuffs. On her head, she wore a knitted beanie that had a large, fluffy pom-pom on top and a pair of earmuffs made of a faux fur. She looked like Holly Hobby and Daniel Boone had borne a child.

To finish off the outfit, Doris accessorized with a large, beaded necklace, a collection of bangles on her wrists, and a vintage, leather satchel that seemed filled to bulging, though Ariel couldn't see with what.

She let loose a loud, cackling laugh that seemed to fill the air around her. "Well? Can you speak?"

Behind Ariel, Katie appeared. "Oh, hi," Katie replied, looking uneasy.

"Why did you stay away for so long?" Doris asked bluntly, looking at Katie and Ariel.

Ariel blanched. "I'm sorry, can we help you?" The mention of her father put Ariel's nerves—already toast from the long trip, lack of heating, and rabid racoon attack—on edge.

"He's out there somewhere," Doris continued, undeterred. "Do you know where?" She pointed one long, bony finger at Katie, who shrank back behind Ariel. Then Doris cackled again, wringing her hands, and sadly said, "You know, he didn't deserve what they did. He didn't do what they say."

Doris shuffled on the crumbling porch, wringing her hands, looking expectantly at Ariel as though Ariel should be able to discern the right answer to the series of bizarre statements. Ariel's heart started to pick up with anxiety even though she didn't feel that Doris was dangerous.

Just the mention of Ariel's father was enough to send her blood pressure climbing.

Katie, having seemingly recovered from the initial shock of Doris's arrival and questioning, looked back out from behind Ariel. "Were you here when Grandpa went missing?"

Ariel stiffened next to her daughter. "I'm sorry," she said softly to the old woman. "He's not here, and we don't know where he is. So, unless you have a good recommendation for pizza that delivers, we'll have to say goodnight and head into town."

Doris shook her head at Ariel, but her eyes were fixed on Katie. "Endless Harbor ain't Miami, okay?"

"Go grab my purse and keys, Katiebug," Ariel said, nodding back toward the house. "Goodnight, Doris." And with that, Ariel closed the door, her stomach churning, wondering what the heck was going on that her idyllic idea of coming home was turning so quickly into a strange nightmare.

***

Ariel navigated the unfamiliar streets of Endless Harbor, with Katie riding shotgun. She could feel her nerves fraying further. Contrary to what she remembered as a quaint, seaside village in her youth, the town now seemed to consist of many more decrepit, old, coastal houses, their paint chipped, and windows boarded up, that loomed in ramshackle disarray over the road like ominous sentinels. The smell of saltwater and fish filled the air as they passed by a fish processing plant just a few miles outside of town. And the only pizza place in Endless Harbor was located inside a gas station, which reeked of stale oil and cigarettes.

Echoes of the words of the strange old woman who'd appeared on their porch were occupying Ariel's thoughts. It was only when Katie spoke beside her that Ariel snapped out of her reverie.

"Mom, this place is creepy. It looks like something out of a horror movie," Katie complained, turning her nose up at the rundown houses they passed by on their way away from Qwik-and-Go Fuel.

"It's not that bad, sweetie. It's just *different* from what you're used to in Miami." Ariel tried to console her daughter, but she could see the skepticism in Katie's eyes. And, really, she was also trying to console herself. The town seemed divided—much more so than when Ariel had been young. The run-down houses were a contrast to the gleaming, expensive boats in the marina. There was still life in Endless Harbor, but when had it separated so drastically?

Downtown was small and unassuming, consisting of small shops, a post office, hardware store, ice cream shop, a bar, and a few restaurants.

"How about we try that food truck over there?" Ariel suggested, pointing to a brightly painted truck parked on the side of the road. "They make amazing lobster rolls in Maine."

But Katie shook her head. "I don't want seafood, Mom. I want a burger. We've had them like a million times already on the drive here. No one can mess up a burger. Reliable. *Familiar*."

Ariel tried to hide her disappointment, and she certainly didn't miss the implication in her daughter's words. She had been looking forward to trying the local seafood, but it seemed Katie was determined to stick to familiar foods. "Okay, fine. We'll go to the diner then."

They ended up eating on the back patio of the only diner in town, The Throwback Diner, which faced the harbor across the street. They sat in a warm island of heat provided by outdoor propane heaters, and though they both kept their coats on, it was comfortable enough. Ariel didn't want to eat inside. After their strange run-in with Doris, she'd had enough of meeting the locals for one night. Maybe she'd feel friendlier in the light of a new day, but for now, she didn't feel like being a social butterfly.

After they'd placed their orders and the waitress had departed, Ariel looked out at the new marina built across the way, the one that hadn't existed when Ariel had lived here last. She tried to enjoy the moment of tranquility. Of course, there had been all of the really big unpleasantness happening once they'd arrived, but there was still a bright side to be found.

Ariel was struck by the beauty of the scene before her. The gilded glow over the water illuminated the sleek lines of the new yachts docked there. The boats seemed to be made of liquid gold as the setting sun hit their surfaces. The dock was empty of people, but the newness of the marina was obvious. Even from across the street, the wood still had that fresh smell, and the ropes that swung at either side of each dock were not frayed, nor faded, and they were tight.

The marina itself was a wide, open space. The yachts were lined up in a neat row, bobbing gently with the movement of the water, each one more impressive than the last. Ariel could see that the marina had been designed with care and attention to detail, from the well-maintained walkways to the strategically placed lights that would make it a beautiful place to be at night. This new marina would bring more tourists and more business to the small, coastal town during season. And many of those tourists might want lodging—a sorely lacking commodity, if her hotel search was any indication—or a meal that wasn't presented to them beside a rack of chewing gum and cigarette lighters.

Their waitress, Jill, returned with their food. She was bubbly and friendly, with a bright smile that seemed to light up her entire face. She was around Ariel's age, and Ariel was grateful for her contagious energy that made it impossible not to feel at ease in her presence. They sure could use some positivity after the day they'd had.

Jill wore a traditional diner uniform, a pink, polo shirt and black slacks, with a white apron tied around her waist. Her hair was styled in a messy bun, and she had a pen tucked behind her ear. She seemed to be the type of person who knew everyone in town. Ariel watched as she bounced between the inside of the diner and the patio, making conversation with her customers easily. She moved efficiently and gracefully, balancing plates and cups with ease. Her presence in the diner seemed to give the place a more homely and friendly feel. It was the atmosphere that Ariel wanted for the sprawling, old Victorian that she'd now taken on. She wanted to create a place that people wanted to be.

Ariel and Katie began to eat, and Ariel's attention was inexorably drawn back to the sight of the new marina across the street. She leaned over to Jill, who was clearing coffee mugs from the next table over, and asked, "Excuse me, can you tell me about the yachts across the way? They're beautiful."

The waitress grinned. "Oh yes, those are all from tourists. Even though it's winter, the new mayor's been working hard to bring more tourism to the area and revitalize it. It's really starting to take off! Season should be hopping this year."

Katie's attention suddenly shifted from her food to something across the street. Ariel followed her daughter's gaze and saw a group of teenagers walking by the marina. Among them was a tall, handsome boy who had apparently caught Katie's eye. The boy looked up and met Katie's gaze and gave her a small, friendly wave.

The boy was striking—athletic but lean, standing at least a head taller than his friends. He had dark, messy hair that was just long enough to fall into his eyes, which were squinted into the fading light in a way that prevented Ariel from being able to discern their color. He wore a navy-blue winter jacket, which was unzipped to reveal a plain white t-shirt underneath. He had on a pair of faded blue jeans that cuffed around a pair of black Converse that looked worn in. He carried himself with a casual confidence, and he had an easy smile that he flashed at Katie as their eyes met.

Ariel could see the faint blush creeping up Katie's cheeks and knew that her daughter was mildly embarrassed, but also a little excited by the attention from the boy. Ariel held back any outward reaction at the twinge of amusement she felt—nothing like the attention of a boy to add another U-turn in her daughter's rapidly changing demeanor. As the group of teenagers walked away, Katie's attention returned to her food, and the two of them continued their meal, Ariel saying nothing.

There was, as she ate, a thin hope that, just maybe, this encounter could be the start of something for Katie. After all, Ariel had treasured her friends from Endless Harbor. If Katie could make new friends, she could leave behind all the mean-girl trouble in Miami and start fresh. Ariel was sure of it.

But she wouldn't push for now. There was neutral territory to cover, and after Jill's info, Ariel was excited by the thought of more tourists coming. She leaned over toward Katie, hoping that she might be encouraged into conversation, and said, "So, this new marina is going to bring in more business. It's a great opportunity for us."

Katie just shrugged, her attention seemingly elsewhere again. She took a half-hearted bite of her burger. Gone was the small kindling of interest and solidarity that had been in her eyes previously. Ariel was quickly losing her again. "That's great, Mom."

Ariel's excitement deflated a bit, but she reminded herself that this move was not just about Katie, it was also about her *own* dreams and aspirations. She would just have to work on getting her daughter excited about the potential that Endless Harbor and Leeside held. It was going to take more than a few yachts and a new marina to change Katie's mind about their new home.

CHAPTER NINE

As Ariel and Katie walked down by the harbor after their dinner, the salty sea air filling their lungs, Ariel noticed that her daughter's sour expression had suddenly dissipated. She followed Katie's gaze to see the group of teenagers from the harbor in the distance just beyond the block where the hardware store was. Ariel smiled to herself, glad that *something* had managed to cheer her daughter up, even if it was just a momentary crush.

"The tall one was cute. And I saw him smile at you," Ariel said, bumping shoulders with her daughter. "He looks nice."

"Thanks, Mom," Katie said, rolling her eyes but still staring at the group of boys.

"Just remember, it's not *just* about looks. That's gotten me in plenty of trouble—handsome can be a one-way ticket to heartbreak city. It's much more important to find someone who respects and treats you well."

Katie rolled her eyes again. "I know, *Mom*. Can we just not talk about anything embarrassing? This is the first time I've felt normal since we left Miami."

Ariel threw up her hands in surrender and fell silent. A few minutes down the main street of Endless Harbor, the small-town hardware store's front door came into view. It was a quaint, red-brick building nestled between a barber shop and a bait-and-tackle store. The windows were adorned with signs advertising various tools and hardware, and a large, wooden sign above the door read "Endless Harbor Hardware Co."

As they approached the store, Ariel remembered their predicament with the broken boiler back at the house. She turned to Katie and suggested, "Hey, why don't we ask the store owner for help? Maybe he knows a heating contractor in the area." Katie, who had been scanning the street, presumably for the group of teenage boys, shrugged and followed her mother inside.

The store was dimly lit and filled with the scent of sawdust and metal. Rows of tools and hardware lined the walls, and a large counter spanned the back of the store. Behind the counter, an older man with a thick, gray beard was counting out the till. He looked up as they approached and gave them a friendly smile.

"Good evening, ladies. How can I help you?" he asked.

"Good evening, sir. We just moved into my father's old house, and the boiler isn't working. Do you know of any heating contractors in the area who could help us out? I know it's probably after hours."

He nodded sympathetically and said, "I'm sorry to hear that. Unfortunately, you're right. Most of the contractors in the tri-county are closed for the evening. But I can loan you an industrial space heater for the night. It's not much, but it'll keep you warm until morning."

"Thank you so much. We'd really appreciate it," Ariel said. She calculated where they could set up a heater—maybe in the living room, and she and Katie could simply camp out there until morning? They could take some of the old rugs from the downstairs bedrooms and tack them up in each of the entryways to the living room.

Just call Charlie.

Ariel batted away the thought. She didn't want to call Charlie and admit defeat this early on. She would stick it out for one night and figure out a better solution in the morning.

The man smiled. "The name's Bob Jenkins. It's no problem at all. It's always tough moving into a new place, especially one that needs some fixing up. I'll be right back."

He disappeared into the dusty recess of the store and was back in minutes, carrying the heater. "It's little but mighty. Hope it helps."

When she took it from him, Ariel gushed again, "This is so kind of you. We can't thank you enough."

The store owner chuckled. "Don't mention it. I'm happy to help out a new neighbor," he said with a smile. He handed Katie a small bag with some extra bulbs for the heater. "You might need these too. Let me know if you need anything else."

With a wave, Ariel hefted the space heater closer to her chest, and she and Katie walked out of the store and back toward the car with the space heater in tow. Katie turned as they came out onto the sidewalk, still stealing glances at the group of boys who were hanging at the street corner in the distance.

Their path back to the SUV took them back by the harbor. The town looked nice lit up, now that it was dark, and some of the shabbiness was disguised by the darkness and the strings of lights strung here and there. The ambience couldn't do anything for the fish smell, but Ariel could almost ignore it now.

The temperature was dropping noticeably now that it was fully dark out, and a bitter winter wind whipped through their hair. The marina lights glowed the brightest of any they'd passed, and Ariel noticed a man working on one of the boats docked there. He was tall and well-built, his muscles flexing as he worked with a grace that seemed untouched by the cold. His ruggedly handsome features were set in a determined expression. Despite the freezing temperatures, he was dressed in only a light sweater and a pair of jeans, seemingly unaffected by the salt wind. In fact, his sleeves were pushed up to his elbows, and Ariel felt momentarily giddy at the girlish twinge of attraction that warmed her as she watched him, his focus and skill captivating her.

But as much as she found him attractive, Ariel looked away when a wave of guilt and confusion gripped her. It was her first day in Endless Harbor, and she was still reeling from her recent breakup with Dylan. The last thing she needed was to be attracted to someone new, especially now.

It couldn't hurt, however, to make friends—right? Just like she had told Katie. Ariel decided to introduce herself to the stranger.

No ulterior motives, she thought wryly.

"Excuse me," she said as they drew up beside him and the gently rocking boat. "I was wondering how in the world you could be comfortable out here working in the cold. Aren't you freezing?"

The man looked up from his work and smiled at Ariel. He had even, white teeth and a wide, friendly grin. "Oh, I've got cold seawater for blood. At least, that's what my dad always said. But thanks for your concern …" He trailed off, and Ariel realized he was asking her name.

"Ariel Hawthorne. This is my daughter Katie. We're renovating the Victorian just east of town, the one on the bluffs. We'll be sending our bed and breakfast guests down to the marina soon, I suspect." Ariel set the space heater down on the sidewalk by her feet and held out a hand for a handshake.

"Oh." He looked at her offered hand for a moment before taking it. His fingers were warm, despite the outside temperature.

"I thought you said you had cold blood," she teased. "Your hands aren't cold at all."

His hazel eyes sparkled. "Miles Clemens. I'm the manager of this marina. It's nice to meet you."

Ariel smiled wider, feeling a sizzle of connection, and allowing it for the briefest moment before she reigned it back in. Miles's expression quickly turned serious, and though he held her hand a moment past what was strictly polite, when he dropped her fingers from his, Ariel felt the absence of his touch.

"I'm afraid that's not going to be an easy feat, opening a bed and breakfast here," he said. "The mayor is pushing for a big, high-end spa resort on the other side of town, and they've been shooting down all the competition. In fact, they bought up a lot of land on your side of the county recently. I'm surprised you held on. Lots of real estate sharks—developers, lawyers—crawling that side of town lately."

Something about his words stuck in Ariel's mind. *Hmm. Lawyers?*

"Surely, there's room for more than one type of accommodation," Ariel replied. "I mean, not every traveler can afford to stay at a high-end resort. Don't you think everyone deserves the chance to enjoy the coast?"

Miles's serious expression turned downright grim. "Miss Hawthorne, you're new in town—"

"Well, I grew up here," she cut in. "But it's been years."

He nodded curtly. "Those years have seen a lot of money leave Endless Harbor, and folks around here are eager to see that money come back. I'm not saying that I'm for it, but the resort's almost a sure thing. And you didn't hear it from me, but you might find yourself waging an uphill battle if you're set on your B&B."

Katie snorted beside her, but Ariel held up a hand to caution her outspoken daughter from making a social misstep—at least this early in their residency. They could go to battle once they had more information.

Ariel felt anger rise in her. She couldn't believe that the town was planning to only cater to the wealthy and shut out regular people like her and her family had been when she'd been young and carefree on these very beaches. Who was this new mayor, and would he be a problem for Ariel?

"Thank you for the warning, Miles," she said, trying to hide her disappointment. "But I'm not one to give up that easily. And I'll be here for the foreseeable future, so you can call me Ariel."

The sparkle returned to his eyes. "Ariel, it is."

"Miles, have a good night." With that, she picked the space heater back up and spun, tilting her head to indicate that Katie should follow.

Once they were out of earshot of Miles, Katie turned a sour expression on Ariel. It reminded Ariel so strongly of the same face that she used to make as a toddler when she didn't get her way that she had to stifle a laugh as Katie groused, "Mom, gross. You didn't have to flirt with that guy while I just stood there like a captive audience!"

Ariel failed in her restraint, and the laugh slipped out. "Oh, Katie, I was just trying to gather information about the town. You know, research on the competition."

"Riiight," Katie said. "Oh, Miles, your hands are so warm ..." Katie jostled against her mother, their shoulders bumping, just like Ariel had instigated earlier.

They reached the car, and Ariel loaded the heater in the back, a small, secret smile touching her lips. "Let's go home, honey."

It was time for sleep, for rest. Ariel would have a new day tomorrow to figure out how to tackle Endless Harbor, the house of many horrors, and the new and possibly *interesting* Miles Clemens.

CHAPTER TEN

"Get your butts in my van!"

The voice made Ariel smile—no small feat, since she was freezing despite the car heater, disgruntled, about as bone-tired as she could get, and ready to collapse. Judging by Katie's weary expression, her daughter felt the same way.

As Ariel and Katie had walked the streets of Endless Harbor, the cold winter air had seeped into her bones, and Ariel had been looking forward to getting inside the house for the night and hopefully warming up. That was, if they could make a successful second trip down to the basement and get the right breaker flipped to turn the power on to get juice to the heater.

Ariel had shuddered, thinking of the mutant raccoon.

But as they'd approached Leeside, winding up the driveway, Ariel and Katie had been greeted with the sight of Charlene's minivan parked in the driveway. The engine was running, and warm heat was pouring out of the open sliding door.

"Get your butts in my van!" Charlene repeated as she opened her own door and climbed out, a big grin on her face.

Ariel was both surprised and relieved to see her sister. They climbed out of their car, leaving that small, warm spot, and Katie rushed her aunt, jumping on her and hugging her tight.

"Oh my goodness, you're freezing!" Charlene exclaimed, embracing her niece. "Come here, both of you. Get in a seat and buckle your seatbelts. Ari, you have your purse? Lock your car. We're going to my house for the night."

Katie sprinted toward the minivan as Ariel and Charlie embraced. They hugged one another tightly, and Ariel could feel the warmth from the minivan envelop them.

"What are you doing here, Charlene?" Ariel asked, still clinging to her sister.

"I tried to call you an hour ago, but your phone went straight to voicemail," Charlene said, not really answering the question.

Ariel looked at her phone. "Huh. Could it be that, among its other charms, Endless Harbor also has cell phone reception issues?"

Charlie laughed. "Oh, yes. The cell towers here are not the most reliable. Anyway, I showed up here and used my key to go inside. I thought you hadn't arrived yet, and I was going to get the heat going to warm up the house and put some stuff in the fridge so you guys could get by in the morning. But the boiler isn't working. Nor is the electricity. I'm sorry Kurt didn't have time to get out here and get this place started up for you guys. The move happened so fast!"

A sigh escaped Katie, loud enough that Ariel could hear it from where she stood, outside the van still. "We found that out," Katie said sourly. "You know what's nice and warm? Miami."

Ariel shot her daughter a look of annoyance. Her temples were throbbing, a headache threatening. There was a part of her that wanted to tell Charlie that they could come over tomorrow and visit. But the part that was a Florida-transplant popsicle and just wanted a soft place to sleep and maybe some tomato soup and a grilled cheese for breakfast in her time of stress wanted to dive into the van and beg to be taken home to Charlie's house.

"I couldn't let my baby sister and niece freeze to death on their first night back in town," Charlene replied, giving Ariel a playful shove toward the open door of the minivan. "Now, come on. I've got the heater on high in there and some hot cocoa waiting for us at my place."

Ariel sighed heavily. "Ok. But I have to grab our overnight bags from the car. The rest of our stuff will be here in a few days from Florida, but we have a couple duffels in the trunk."

"Go on, get 'em."

It was moments later, two bags in hand, that Ariel gratefully climbed into the minivan. Charlene looked back over the driver's seat and noticed the space heater that Ariel had stashed in the van before she'd gone for the bags. "What's that for?" she asked.

"Well, since the boiler in the house isn't working, we went into town to try to find a repairman. We knew it was a longshot at this time of day. But there was a nice man at the hardware store who lent us this. I don't want to leave it and risk something happening. He was so kind to loan it," Ariel said sheepishly.

Charlene shook her head and rolled her eyes. "You should have called me immediately when you came into town. Kurt was home all afternoon! He could have come over." Charlie clicked her tongue as she looked at the house. "I can't believe you really wanted this dump."

"I didn't want to bother you," Ariel said, buckling her seatbelt as Charlie began to ease down the driveway. "You didn't have to come check up on us." She bristled inside at Charlie's classification of the house—yes, it might be a dump, but it was a dump that now belonged to Ariel. And it represented a fresh, new start for Ariel and Katie and the long-forgotten property. She was tired, and maybe a little emotional from the past few weeks, but Charlie's comment stung a little harder than Ariel knew her sister had intended.

"We just got here," Ariel protested weakly. "And we thought we could make it. You didn't want me to do this in the first place, and now here we are, already failing. No heat."

"Yeah, you just got here. But you're leaving with me, sister. This place is a death trap without heating," Charlene insisted. "Besides, I want to hear all about your trip and catch up."

Katie, who had been quiet until now, chimed in, "And we have to tell you about the racoon that chased us."

Charlene's eyes widened in surprise and concern. "A racoon? Oh, no. You definitely can't stay here tonight. Let's add to our tasks for tomorrow the heater and calling an exterminator in the morning."

"Thanks for coming to rescue us, Aunt Charlie," Katie said. Ariel bristled again. Katie's mood had swung so wildly on the trip, and Ariel herself had not been the recipient of very much of the appreciation that she now heard in her daughter's voice. Again, she took a steadying breath, knowing that she was not in the best headspace. In fact, she was downright burned out.

Charlie scoffed softly. "I came by because I wanted to make sure you were settled in okay. But from the looks of it, that's not the case. I love you both, and you're staying with me tonight. No argument. We'll come back in the morning and figure out all the things necessary to make this place habitable."

Katie giggled. "Aunt Charlie sounds like you when I don't wake up on time, Mom," she observed.

"That's called the mom voice, and it's a universal tone," Charlie explained, managing to get the van turned around at a wide spot in the driveway so that she could point the vehicle straight toward the two-lane road that ran at the end of it. She flipped her blinker on and looked at Ariel in the rearview mirror. "Sit back and let yourself be cared for, missy."

Grateful tears filled Ariel's eyes, and she swiped at them as they coasted down the highway toward Charlie's place.

Katie reached over and put her hand on Ariel's arm.

Ariel sat back and let herself be cared for.

***

Back at Charlene's house, Ariel and Katie were no sooner out of the minivan than they were set upon by a mob. Out of the house came Charlene's husband Kurt, their two kids, and the family dog—Rufus, a Great Dane who Ariel had only seen pictures of.

Pictures did not do Rufus justice.

As the creature got closer, Ariel braced herself. The dog was massive, with a shiny, black coat and a wagging tail—and the tip of his wagging tail was almost as tall as Ariel. As soon as the Great Dane spotted Ariel, he let out a joyful bark and took off running toward her. Ariel couldn't help but laugh as the dog jumped up on her, its paws landing on her shoulders as it licked her face affectionately.

"Rufus, down!" Kurt shouted from the front porch, but the dog paid no attention to him. It was too busy showering Ariel with love and affection. Ariel was overwhelmed by the dog's energy, but at the same time, she admittedly felt a little envious of the unbridled joy and excitement that Rufus seemed to exude. As Rufus settled down, Ariel petted him, giving him a good scratch behind the ears, and hugged the dog tightly. Rufus moved onto Katie, who was quickly bowled over onto the soft snow on the front lawn, and she giggled and shrieked as Rufus bombarded her with kisses.

Charlene came out of the van just as Kurt reached it, and the spouses shared a hug. Kurt howled when Charlie pressed her cold nose into his warm neck, and she laughed as he set her away from him, a mock-scowl on his face.

"Woman, you're as bad as Rufus." His face split into a grin as he turned to Ariel. "Hi, kiddo."

Ariel grinned back at her brother-in-law and then was pulled into a strong hug.

Kurt, in his mid-forties, definitely rocked his rugged and weathered appearance. He had a thick, salt-and-pepper beard that was well-groomed and gave him a distinguished look. He was tall and broad-shouldered, with a muscular build that hinted at a lifetime spent working with his hands. His hair was short and wavy, and his deep-set blue eyes seemed to twinkle with a hint of mischief. He had a friendly smile and a warm, outgoing personality, and he always seemed to have a kind word or a joke to share. Despite his rough exterior, he had a gentle and caring nature, and he was deeply devoted to his family, particularly his wife Charlene. Ariel had always liked him, ever since he'd showed up as a less rugged teenager on the front porch of the

48

Victorian with a bouquet of wildflowers for Charlie—and never seemed to leave.

When Kurt released her, Ariel turned to see that Rufus was now on the lawn with three kids—Katie, Peter, and Hannah—and he was in heaven with all the attention. Hannah was scratching his ears, Peter his belly, and Katie was scrunching a spot under his arm that was making one of his back legs pump.

"Hi, offspring," Charlie said. "I'm home."

Peter looked up and rolled his eyes. "We know, Mom. How else would Aunt Ariel and Katie be here?"

Peter was eight, bespectacled, and as geeky as they came. Ariel adored how her young nephew could rattle off comic book facts and video game lore in an encyclopedic way, but that wasn't always something his total opposite, sporty (and beleaguered), older sister appreciated. And, apparently, the whole kid-put-upon-by-parent attitude was a thing here too.

Ariel chuckled. "So, it's not just me that gets the eyerolls."

"It's sweeping the nation, I guess," Charlie said, sighing. "Kurt, can you get the bags?"

"On it."

As Kurt went to the van to retrieve their luggage, Ariel went inside with Charlie and the kids.

Hannah slid up beside Ariel and gave her a big side hug. "Aunt Ariel, will you come to the stables and see me ride horses this week?"

"Oh, maybe, honey." Ariel looked down at Hannah, who at twelve, looked so much like a young Charlie that it was eerie. Where Peter had Kurt's fair skin and features, Hannah was every bit Charlie's olive tone and the big, dark eyes that were the trademark of both Charlie and Ariel. "It depends on the house, okay?"

"Yay! Okay!" Hannah turned to Katie and Peter. "You guys want to go watch TV?"

Katie, Hannah, and Peter immediately zoomed off with Rufus upstairs, happily chattering and leaving a trail of shoes and coats behind them on the staircase.

As Ariel walked into Charlene's living room, she was immediately struck by the cozy, welcoming atmosphere of the space. The room was decorated in a coastal bungalow style, with honey-colored wood paneling and white-washed walls. The open concept layout allowed the kitchen to flow seamlessly into the family room, where a large sectional couch faced a TV. The smell of soup simmering on the stove added to the homey feel of the room. Soft blankets were draped over the back of the couch, inviting anyone to curl up and relax. The room was not overly large, but it felt just the right size—not too cramped and not too spacious. It was a perfect space to spend a relaxing evening with friends and family.

Charlie, who had hung her coat up by the front door and hustled into the kitchen, lifted the lid on the large pot that sat on the stove and called to Ariel, "Take your jacket off! Sit!"

Kurt bustled in the front door, dropping the bags by the coat rack and taking off his boots. As Ariel shrugged off her coat, he stepped over to take it from her and hang it up.

"Heard we were getting a hard freeze tonight," he said. "We might not be out at the jobsite in the morning. If so, I can go out and look at the heat at Leeside."

"Leeside!" Ariel laughed, surprised by the old moniker. "I haven't heard that name for the place since my dad was around."

"Leeside at the Seaside," Charlene sing-songed, just like Dad used to. "Oh my goodness, that house is a disaster," Charlene exclaimed, stirring the pot—in more ways than one, as far as Ariel was concerned. "It's going to take a lot of work to get it up to livable standards."

Kurt nodded in agreement. "Yeah, it's definitely a fixer upper. I mean, it was a fixer upper five years ago. Ten years ago."

Ariel sighed as she sunk into the soft, cozy sectional. "I know, but I'm dead set on making it work. I *will* turn it into a bed and breakfast. And I will cook there, just like I used to, when I was happy and fulfilled and not forced to put up with the likes of a spoiled, nepotism baby of a CEO."

She didn't miss when Charlene and Kurt exchanged worried glances. Kurt plopped down on the sectional diagonal from Ariel. "You should know that the mayor is buying up land to build a high-end spa resort on the other side of town," he said. "He's been pushing out small business owners like you intend to be."

"Yep. I heard that from Miles Clemens at the marina," Ariel said. "Almost verbatim. Still doesn't faze me." A thought struck Ariel. "Oh, hey. Richard Holcomb, did you ask him what he called me about?"

Charlie raised her ladle and waved it. "Yes! Perfect timing. How funny you ask now. He was contacted with an offer on Leeside, an offer to buy it out for the very same development project that we're discussing."

Ariel felt her eyes widen. "He wants to buy it?"

"A third party, probably Stanton or his associates. But I turned him down—you wanted the house."

"Oh. Well, was it a lot of money?" Not that she would sell, but she was curious.

Charlene nodded as she started ladling soup into bowls across the kitchen counter. "It was not a small amount. You can look at the offer if you want. But it you're forging ahead with the renovation, then the mayor *is* going to put up a fight against your bed and breakfast. He wants to turn Endless Harbor into a tourist destination for the wealthy only."

Charlene added, "And the town is pretty worried about what that spa resort will do to the small-town charm of Endless Harbor. I mean, progress is nice, but who wants the Throwback Diner replaced by two cookie-cutter coffee shops at opposite corners of the same intersection? But the townsfolk never have a say in the matter. We'll see what happens."

A knot formed in Ariel's stomach. "What can I do then? I can't just give up on my dream. I'm committed. Or maybe I should be."

"You'll need to take up the fight at City Hall," Kurt suggested. "Go there first thing on Monday morning and make your case. The issue is that feet are dragging on operating licenses and such. You might have luck on the building permits getting approved. They don't much care if you improve the house, I suspect. But the second you start letting it out that you intend to run the place as an inn, you'll be on Richard Stanton's radar."

Ariel nodded determinedly. "So, Stanton is the new mayor? The villain of the piece? I will go visit City Hall. Is there somewhere I can look to start interviewing contractors to help me with the house? Kurt, do you have any spare guys?"

But Kurt shook his head. "I'm sorry Ariel, but my crew is tied up for the next three months on an apartment complex job in the next county. And as for solo handymen, every tradesman in the area has already been hired by the mayor to work on his resort. You're going to have a hard time finding someone to help you."

Ariel lifted her chin. "Then I'll handle it myself."

Another worried look passed between her sister and brother-in-law as Charlene began to bring dinner to the long, eat-in counter that made up the near side of the kitchen island.

"Let's worry about it tomorrow," Charlene said. "Did you guys eat?"

"We did, but—" Ariel looked down at the steaming bowl of tomato soup, just what she had planned to eat for breakfast the next morning. It seemed even better now. A plate with a perfectly toasted, buttery grilled cheese slid next to her bowl. "This looks so, so good."

Ariel dug in as Charlie called upstairs to let the kids know that food was ready. Her thoughts were already spinning toward tomorrow. She hoped that worrying would turn into solving, and that she would find Mayor Stanton less of an adversary than he was rumored to be.

CHAPTER ELEVEN

Ariel was ready to take on her opponent.

A hot, hearty dinner, followed by a good night's sleep, topped off with a luscious breakfast of maple oatmeal and sausages did Ariel and Katie a world of good. In fact, Ariel was surprised to see Katie actually bouncing as she came down the stairs to breakfast.

Now, they were bundled back up and off to the hardware store again. When Ariel and Katie walked into the quaint, cluttered shop, the owner, Bob, the kind-looking older man with a thick, gray beard who had helped them the night before, recognized them immediately from their visit the previous evening.

"Ah, you're the ones with the broken boiler, right?" he said with a smile. "I hope that space heater kept you warm last night. How are things at the old Victorian?"

Ariel explained that they were making progress, but they were still having trouble with the boiler. "I'm sure the heater works great—thank you so much," Ariel said. "But we ended up crashing at my sister's, so we'll bring it back tomorrow, if that's okay. We're just here to grab some supplies to fix up the house."

Ariel looked at the list that Kurt had given her. When she frowned at the list, the owner laughed and held out his hand. "Hand it here."

She handed the paper over, and he seemed to know exactly what the list meant.

As Bob gathered her materials, moving from aisle to aisle with Ariel and Katie following, his expression turned serious. He asked, "Are you sure you know what you're getting yourself into? The mayor's got big plans for this town, and I'm not sure it'll be easy to compete."

"What kind of plans?" Ariel asked, her curiosity piqued. Of course, she'd heard from both Miles and Kurt about the resort, but maybe there was a detail that Bob had that the others hadn't. She knew playing dumb wasn't entirely her strong suit, but maybe this fellow had information that she could use to her advantage.

"Oh, he's caused quite the stir in the community. Some folks are excited for the potential boost to tourism that all his proposed developments would bring, but others worry it'll change things too much. In fact, there's a small rebel faction out there who are trying their best to get up opposition to the whole deal."

That's new information, Ariel thought.

"You're out at Leeside, right? Lee Briggs was your daddy?"

Ariel felt queasy as he said *was your daddy*, as though her father were dead. "He is my father, yes," she said. She could feel Katie watching her, watching the exchange. "And thank you for the warning," she said with a determined smile. "But I'm not going to give up that easily."

Bob studied her for a moment, perhaps expecting that she was going to say more. Ariel just lifted her chin and stayed silent.

Mr. Jenkins gave her an encouraging smile. "I have no doubt you'll make it work. And if you need any more help or advice, don't hesitate to come back and ask."

They followed Bob to the front, where he rang them up and passed over a large paper bag weighed down with supplies. Ariel rolled down the top and stashed it in the oversized canvas bag she had brought just for that purpose. With another thanks for the loan of the heater, Ariel and Katie left the shop.

The queasiness intensified. She had worked so hard to put her broken heart behind her and start anew, but now it seemed like her dreams of a successful B&B were going to be thwarted by the mayor's plan. But she was determined to make it work.

As they took their supplies and headed back to the house, Ariel thought about her father, her chest tightening. One day, he was talking to her about revamping the greenhouse in the backyard of Leeside. The next, he was gone from their lives—his old sedan gone, his credit cards and every other trace of him inactive for the years since.

She pushed the pain away, mulling over in her head instead what Bob had said—there was a rebel faction in Endless Harbor? If so, how did she find them?

***

Ariel had never been the handy one in her family. When something broke in her old house, she was always the first to volunteer to call a repair service to fix it. So, when the lock on one of the doors in her father's old house wouldn't turn, Ariel felt less than confident that she could handle it. But now, bag full of spray lubricant and rubber mallet and whatever else Kurt had asked her to get for the boiler, Ariel was armed and ready to try, at least.

She dug through the toolbox she had found in the basement—a scary trip that had involved flashbacks to the racoon attack—pulling out a screwdriver, a hammer, and a set of pliers. The lock was old and rusted, but Ariel was determined to get it working again.

The living room of the old Victorian house was dimly lit, with tall bay windows on either side of the room letting in streams of sunlight. The walls were in sore need of a fresh coat of paint, with ornate crown molding and baseboards that Ariel knew would stand out in a crisp white. The hardwood flooring was worn but still gleamed with a hint of its former grandeur. A fireplace with a marble mantel dominated one wall, with a large painting of a countryside scene hanging above it. A set of French doors led to a small porch overlooking the garden. The furniture was a mix of antique and modern pieces, with a plush velvet couch and armchairs in shades of deep purple and navy, right alongside the old recliner that her dad had loved. Ariel didn't have the heart to take that old recliner out. A large bookshelf filled with an eclectic collection of books and trinkets stood in one corner, and an upright piano sat in another. The room had a musty, old-world charm that was both inviting and slightly eerie at the same time.

She undid the screws holding the lock in place, pried the hardware off the door, and set to work, carefully removing the rusted pins and cleaning them up. She replaced them with new ones she had picked up at the hardware store earlier that day and reassembled the lock, giving it a good test turn to make sure it was working properly before she attempted to put it back on the door.

Feeling proud of her accomplishment, Ariel hung the lock back on the door and stepped back to admire her handiwork. But as soon as she let go of the door, it fell off its hinges with a loud crash. Ariel jumped back to avoid being hit by the door, and her heart sank as she looked at the door, now lying flat on the ground. She could see where the ancient wood of the door frame had splintered, causing the hinges to give way.

This whole place felt ready to crash down around her ears.

"I can't believe it," Ariel muttered to herself, feeling a wave of frustration and disappointment wash over her. "I should have known better. This house is falling apart!"

"I told you!"

Ariel spun at the sound of her sister's voice. Charlie stood in the open front door, the handle of a wheeled cooler in her hand.

"You eavesdropped too soon," Ariel said, sputtering. "I was about to say *good thing I have the patience to fix it all*."

Charlie grinned. "Well, how about a break, oh saintly sister of mine, for a sandwich and some potato salad?"

Ariel was actually famished. She picked up the door and leaned it against the nearby wall, trying to figure out how to fix it. But it was clear that it was beyond her capabilities. She wouldn't admit that to Charlie, though. She'd just search up a DIY video later on and learn what she needed to do—after her sister left. As soon as she made her plan, though, Ariel felt a twinge of guilt. Charlie hadn't been unreasonably mean-spirited about Leeside—it was a hot mess. It was really Ariel's pride that kept her from agreeing with her sister's *correct* assessment of the old place.

"Food sounds so good. Your husband is down in the racoon maze of doom getting the electricity and heating working. Should we throw down a sandwich? I'm afraid the racoons will eat it. If they haven't already had their fill eating him."

"I texted him that I was here. Nothing like the siren call of turkey and provolone to pry him away from the intriguing puzzle of the malfunctioning boiler. He said the electric is just a busted breaker. Should be easy to fix with this." Charlie held up a paper bag from Bob's hardware shop. "New one."

As soon as Charlie said it, Kurt came tromping up the basement stairs. Ariel could hear his heavy boots against the worn treads. Momentarily, his head popped through the doorway between the kitchen and the living room. "Turkey?"

Charlene had already started to unpack lunch onto the coffee table in the living room. She put out two wrapped sandwiches, one on top of the other, and pointed to them. Then she pointed to the paper bag. "Turkey there, breaker there." Kurt happily followed her directions to the stack.

Ariel took the next offered sandwich from Charlie, and Charlie set out a big, plastic bowl of potato salad and a stack of paper plates next to Kurt's sandwiches. Katie, perhaps hearing the same siren song that Kurt had, came down the stairs with a bundle of old curtains in her arms, dust flying off the stack with every careful step that she took down the stairs. When she made it down to the living room, she dropped the bundle unceremoniously and then sneezed three times in a row.

"Eek," Ariel said. "I think I saw brains fly out on that last one."

Katie rubbed at her nose and swiped at her watering eyes. "It's okay. The racoons eat brains. They'll clean it up." Then she bounded toward her aunt, who held a sandwich out to her.

After they were all settled with food, Charlie asked Kurt, "So, what's the diagnosis on the old heat bucket in the dungeon?"

Kurt chewed, swallowed, and said, "It was the racoons. There's a nest down there. Three babies."

Katie shrieked with delight. Charlene's mouth fell open. Ariel almost dropped her sandwich. "You have got to be kidding me. We were down there. We saw nothing!"

Kurt shrugged. "They're inside the boiler. The whole back panel is off and looks like it has been for many years. Wasn't hard for mama to get in. She probably came through the house, to be honest. Lots of gaps up top that would get her into the attic, and from there, it's just a matter of finding the holes that lead down. You're missing heat register vents on both floors, so ..."

"That's why the mama raccoon was so aggressive to us," Katie observed. "She thought we would hurt her babies."

"Well, we gotta evict them," Ariel said. "Right? We can't fix the boiler with live baby racoons in there."

Katie whined, and Charlie reached over and patted her. "Honey, we'll call the local wildlife rescue. They'll take good care of them." Charlie took the last bite of her sandwich, dug her phone out of her pocket, and stood. She started tapping the screen and then wandered out to the porch as soon as a cheery, muffled voice answered.

"So, what has to be done after the animals are out?" Ariel braced for the answer.

"Luckily, it's just old wiring that's prevented the current boiler from working. We'll get the critters out, order a new access panel so that we discourage any more squatters, and I'll get the wiring ordered and rewire it. They won't have the gauge I need in town, so we'll have to wait. You guys stick at our house for now."

Ariel nodded, relieved.

Charlene came back in, a smile on her face. "They'll be out this afternoon to get the babies and set a live trap for mama." She waved her phone. "Kurt, honey, school just called. Hannah has an extra cheer practice tonight, so I gotta run her gym stuff down to the school. You need anything from town?"

As if on cue, Kurt's phone chirped. He swiped to see his messages and then frowned. "Nope. And it looks like they might need me over at the apartment job. Security at the site says there's water free running from one of the mains, and they can't reach the water company." He jumped up from the couch and grabbed his second, still wrapped, sandwich. "I'll go swap this breaker real quick, get the power on so you guys can use that space heater, and then I'll jet."

Ariel stood too. "Thanks for your help, both of you."

"See you at home tonight?" Charlene said.

"Yes. And can I cook dinner?" Ariel had scoped out the three grocery stores in Endless Harbor, and she was fairly confident that at least one would have ingredients she could use to begin practicing some of the menu ideas she had for the B&B.

Charlie grinned. "You haven't cooked for me since I can't remember when."

"Tonight, then?"

"Tonight."

Quick hugs were shared, and Kurt and Charlene were off in two directions.

***

As the sun began to set, Ariel and Katie were both covered in a thick layer of grime and dust, their muscles aching from hours of cleaning. It was obvious that they had barely made a dent in just the clearing out that needed to be done. But the living room was livable, and the fireplace was cleared and clean enough to have housed a warming fire all day, in addition to the now-functioning electricity. Ariel couldn't think about the peeling wallpaper, creaky floorboards, and musty smell that still threatened from almost every other room—insurmountable foes that seemed to mock her efforts.

As they sat down for a break before packing things up for the night and heading back to Charlie's, Ariel fought against a twinge of doubt creeping in. Katie looked exhausted, and she had slipped into sullen silence again as the day had worn on. Ariel had an inkling that it might have something to do with tomorrow being her first day at Endless Harbor High—new place, new people, new school.

"I don't know about you, Katie, but I feel like we're not making much progress here," she said, letting out the frustration in her voice.

Katie, who had been silently staring into the dancing flames in the hearth, looked up at her mother with a look of exhaustion. "I know, Mom. It's just so overwhelming," she said, her voice barely above a whisper.

"The house or high school?"

"Both. I mean, mostly school. It's tomorrow."

58

Ariel could see the fear in her daughter's eyes and knew that it mirrored her own. "I know, sweetie," she said, reaching out to give Katie's hand a reassuring squeeze. "But we can do this. We'll take it one day at a time, one room at a time. One class at a time. And before you know it, this place will be a beautiful bed and breakfast, just like I always dreamed of. And you will be living the teenaged dreams that you only see in TV shows. Please don't start living the one where the girl slays vampires, though. "

But as she spoke the words, Ariel knew that they were easier said than done. She had a vision of turning this house into a successful bed and breakfast, but the reality of the work and the money it would take was starting to weigh on her. She had a fairly substantial savings account, and the house in Miami was drawing multiple bids, but she didn't have so much of a cushion that she could afford to sink renovation costs into Leeside and not recoup them.

Katie, sensing her mother's doubts, gave her a small smile. "I know, Mom. I'm just a little nervous, that's all. What if this doesn't work out? What if we're not happy here like we were in Miami?"

She thought suddenly of Dylan, and how he would probably be trying to talk her out of the whole house adventure if he were here—and not in a loving, concerned way like Charlie. As Ariel sat in the grand living room of *her* stately Victorian home, her mind drifted to a time long ago, when she was still in the thrall of a love that had ultimately proven to be ill-fated. Dylan had always thought he knew better than her, and it was a character trait she'd ignored. He'd had so many other good qualities. But now, the memory of all the times he had argued against her under the guise of "just helping her out with her logic" made her start to simmer inside.

The new, burning desire she had to prove to him that she was capable of success, even without him by her side, joined that anger. Maybe Mitzi was suggestable, and that was why he had so callously dumped Ariel.

And then there was Opulent and the years of dedication that had just been cast aside when she'd been axed from her position. And Katie's trouble with Brittany-the-bully, who had probably continued longer than she would have if Ariel had had time to take care of things properly.

Happy? Miami had actually turned out miserably. Ariel was sure that what Katie was craving wasn't their former city, but the feeling of routine and normalcy that they had cultivated there. Even if in that routine there had been a lot of dysfunction.

Ariel had a sudden, inspired thought. She picked up her phone, opened the internet browser, and did a search for the city government building in Endless Harbor. When she navigated to the page for the mayor's office, she was delighted to see that there was an option to schedule a meeting with the mayor. A few clicks later, and she was surprised again when there was an opening the very next day. She reserved it as fast as her fingers could swipe.

Katie slumped over against Ariel, her head resting on Ariel's shoulder. Ariel tipped her head to the side until their hair touched. She let out a held breath and reached for Katie's hand.

"Sweetie, we'll make it work. I promise. And if it doesn't, we'll figure something else out."

There was no reply, and Ariel looked over to find that Katie had fallen, sound asleep, against her.

CHAPTER TWELVE

As Ariel pulled into the parking lot of the high school the next day, she could feel the tension radiating off of Katie, who was slouching in the passenger seat, staring at the building with a scowl on her face. The school was a large, imposing brick structure, with a tall clock tower that loomed over the surrounding neighborhood.

Katie had been dreading this day for weeks, ever since they had decided to move to Endless Harbor. The move was supposed to be a fresh start for the both of them, but for Katie, Ariel knew it had meant leaving behind her friends and starting at a new school where she knew no one—and that today must feel like an obstacle course she wasn't prepared for.

"Come on, sweetie," Ariel said, trying to inject some cheer into her voice. "It'll be good for you to make some new friends."

"I don't want new friends," Katie grumbled, crossing her arms over her chest. "I want my old friends from Miami. And I hate this stupid school. It's so old and ugly."

Ariel's heart ached for her daughter, who had been through so much in the past year. The move had been hard, and Ariel dreaded adding the stress of struggling to adjust to life in a new town.

As they walked up to the entrance of the school, Ariel could see the other students streaming inside, chatting and laughing with their friends. She could see that Katie was feeling more and more out of place with each step. Katie clutched her backpack tightly, her eyes scanning the building with a mix of fear and disgust. Ariel could see the uncertainty in the way her daughter's shoulders were tense, and how her footstep faltered ever so slightly. She knew that this new chapter in Katie's life would be filled with unknowns. Ariel wanted to be there for her daughter, to support her and guide her through this transition, but she also knew that she had to let Katie navigate this new experience on her own.

With a deep breath and a reassuring smile, Ariel squeezed Katie's hand and whispered, "You got this. You'll be fine." Ariel put her arm around her daughter's shoulders. "I'll be here to pick you up after school, and we'll work on the house together after. I think the wallpaper gets here today. And who knows? Maybe you *will* make some new friends."

"Yeah, right," Katie said, rolling her eyes. "I doubt it. This place is full of weirdos." She pulled away from Ariel as they mounted the front steps.

"Now, that's not true," Ariel said, trying to sound more cheerful than she felt. "Everyone here is just trying to go about their normal routine like we are. And I know it's hard, but I believe in you. You're strong, and you can handle this."

"I guess," Katie said, sounding unconvinced. "But I don't want to be here. I want to be back in Miami with my real friends."

"You hated Miami!" Ariel said, giving her daughter a side hug. Her hugs and squeezes *were* probably getting weird, but Ariel didn't care. She would be that weird mom who hugged too much. "Katie, we're here now, and we're going to make the best of it. Period. Full stop. We're not moving again, even if a hoard of racoons invades the house. Hundreds."

Katie didn't respond, just trudged along beside her mother, her eyes glued to the ground. Fear and apprehension were so clearly etched on her daughter's face. Katie had been bullied at her old school, and it was all too apparent that the thought of going through that again was weighing heavily on her mind—it was written in practical words across her furrowed forehead.

As they walked through the crowded halls, Ariel could see the curious glances that were cast in Katie's direction. She sensed that her daughter was feeling self-conscious and out of place, and she wished she could do something to ease her anxiety. The halls of the high school were a chaotic, bustling maze of students rushing to and fro, books clutched tightly to their chests as they navigated the narrow corridors. The walls were adorned with colorful posters and announcements, and the floors were made of scuffed linoleum that had seen better days.

Lockers lined the walls, their metal doors clanging shut as students grabbed their books and headed to class. The air was thick with the sounds of chatter, laughter, and the occasional screech of a squeaky locker. The smell of a freshly brewed mix of body spray and teen body odor hung in the air, making Ariel's nose wrinkle. The fluorescent lighting overhead flickered, casting a harsh, artificial light over the scene. The energy was high as students were excitedly catching up with friends they hadn't seen since yesterday.

Finally, they reached Katie's first-period class. Ariel hugged her tightly before letting her go. Hug number seventy-two of the morning. Ariel felt like that was a win. Maybe a bit of an exaggeration but still a win. "You're going to do great," she whispered. "I love you."

Katie managed a small smile, but Ariel could tell she was still scared. "I love you, too, Mom," she said finally, before turning and walking into the classroom.

Ariel watched her daughter disappear into the room, her heart heavy with worry.

Katie would make it through—there was no way that this would be Miami all over again.

***

As Ariel walked into the mayor's office after dropping Katie at school, her heart was pounding with anxiety. She had spent hours last night researching the town's regulations and zoning laws, and she felt confident that her bed and breakfast idea was a viable one—considering what was allowable by law in Endless Harbor. However, she knew that the mayor's involvement in the development of the resort would make this an uphill battle, just as Kurt and Charlie had warned.

He didn't have to outright break the law, and he could still keep her tied up in so much red tape that opening her business would become too much of a burden. So, she had to be proactive, or she'd be forced to quit. There was the added complication of her future plan to open the kitchen of the B&B to outside diners and private events, which she was planning on keeping close to the vest for now. One battle at a time. But with money of his own at stake if she proved to be competition, Ariel feared that Stanton might not be receptive to her proposal.

Ariel walked into the grand marble foyer of the mayor's office, her heart pounding with determination. As soon as she entered the waiting area of the mayor's office, though, Ariel knew something was wrong. His secretary caught sight of her and frowned deeply.

She had an appointment, and she wasn't going to let some secretary stand in her way. She approached the desk, a grand affair of polished mahogany, and met the eyes of the woman behind it.

"I'm here to see the mayor," Ariel said, her voice steady. "I have an appointment."

The woman, a severe-looking blonde with a pinched expression, looked at her with disdain. "I'm sorry, but the mayor is unavailable at the moment. Perhaps you could make another appointment?"

Ariel felt her blood boil. "I booked this time. I have important business to discuss with the mayor."

The woman's expression didn't change. "*I'm sorry*, but Mr. Stanton is very busy. He simply cannot see you today." She reached over and picked up a manila folder, handing it out to Ariel. "He sends his regrets and asked me to give this to you."

Ariel took the folder, flipping it open to see form after form after form of building permits and other applications that she would have to get through to open her inn. Ariel could feel her temper rising. "I demand to see him," she said, her voice raised. "He serves the people of Endless Harbor, and I am one of those citizens."

The woman's expression remained deadpan. "Miss, the mayor is not available. You'll have to come back another time."

Ariel bit her lip, trying to steady herself before she snapped back. "Fine," she said, her voice tight. "But I will be back, and I will see the mayor. And when I do, he will regret not seeing me today."

With that, she turned on her heel and stormed out of the office, her mind already whirring with plans for her next move. She wouldn't be deterred so easily, not when her dreams and the future of her business were on the line. As she walked back to her car, she couldn't let go of the feeling that the mayor had eyes in more places in Endless Harbor than Ariel knew about.

CHAPTER THIRTEEN

Ariel had been working on the house for most of the afternoon, trying to tackle one of the many projects that needed to be done—stripping old wallpaper—and distracting herself from the missed meeting with Mayor Stanton. Kurt had dropped by earlier with wire that he'd found at a hardware store in the next county over, a lucky find that allowed them to fix the boiler—which was now raccoon-free—and meant that Ariel and Katie could spend the night at the house for the first time. Luckily, the movers had arrived the day prior, and they had their beds and dressers in place as well. The movers had also hauled away many of the old, decrepit furnishings that had cluttered up the lower floor of Leeside.

Things were looking up.

She was elbow deep in paint when she heard a knock on the door. Wiping her hands on a rag, she made her way to the front door to find Miles, the manager of the marina, standing on the porch.

"Oh. Hi! Uh, Miles, right? What are you—"

"Hey there," he said with a friendly smile. "I wanted to come by and make sure I didn't give you the wrong impression the other day when we first met. I don't want you to think I was being dismissive or rude—it was kind of an off day for me."

Ariel tried not to stare—how was it that he looked so model-perfect? She was suddenly conscious of her grimy clothes and hair. She probably had wallpaper stuck to her somewhere.

Ariel shook her head, reaching up to smooth her hair. "I appreciate you stopping by. That's so kind of you. I didn't think you were rude at all, though."

Miles let out a sigh. "I've been looking for a piece of land to build a boat slip, but I've had no luck because of the mayor's push for the resort. I understand your B&B idea is facing the same roadblock. I thought we might swap ideas to maybe get past the city hurdles?"

Ariel took a minute to study Miles Clemens. He stood tall and windswept, his biceps rippling in a way that only a man who worked with his hands could possess. She marveled again at his lack of a jacket in the cold air. His hazel eyes sparkled with a hint of mischief, and his dark hair was tousled in a way that made Ariel's heart skip a beat. He looked in his early forties, but there was a rugged handsomeness about him that made him appear more youthful, and he made Ariel's knees weak.

Ariel nodded, clearing her throat. "Yeah, I just had a cancelled meeting with the mayor. He's opposed to my plans for the B&B, but I *will not* be easily dissuaded. Even if I have to do it all myself, I'll fix up this house and make it the best darned place to stay in Endless Harbor. If I can find someone to help around here."

Miles grinned. "Well, then, glad I stopped by. You're in luck. I may not be a professional contractor, but I'm pretty handy with a hammer and saw. I'd be happy to help out if you need it."

Ariel felt a sense of relief wash over her. "That would be amazing, thank you." Then an idea struck her. "Listen, why don't you come in? I might have an idea for your boat slip ..."

***

Two hours later, Miles had his boat slip, and Ariel had her handyman. The old property maps of the land surrounding Leeside had been rolled out over the living room coffee table, and she and Miles had pored over them, confirming on several years' worth of surveys that, indeed, there was ocean access that Ariel now owned down at the small beach that bordered Leeside's six acres.

"This is amazing," Miles said. "I mean, more than I could have hoped for. If you'll set up the lease for me, I'll sign it. I don't care what you ask in rent."

Ariel looked over at him. "You mean in addition to your helping around here? I couldn't ask for rent. Just knowing that I'm sticking it to that meddling mayor is plenty extra for me."

Miles's face scrunched. "I insist. It's not in my nature to take advantage of a situation."

Ariel felt her face flame a bit at the way her brain interpreted that. Miles did have some pretty nice lips. And she'd bet that he was a good kisser.

"Ariel?"

She snapped back to reality and waved away his protest. "Handyman services for the first year. We'll negotiate after that, sound good?"

Since he could likely tell that she wouldn't budge, he nodded reluctantly. Then he looked up, and she watched his eyes trace the crown molding. "This place is really great," he said. "I'm glad you're fixing it up. Your dad's old place?"

"Yes. You have family here?"

Miles shook his head. "No, I only came to town a few years ago. I had to get away from my old life," he said, his voice trailing off.

Well, that sounds like he's running from something mysterious, Ariel thought.

Miles rubbed his hands on the kegs of his jeans and stood. "Well, thank you again. I think this will be the start of a beautiful friendship."

Ariel grinned. "Casablanca? Really? Overused."

He shrugged. "It seems fitting. We're by the sea."

Just as Ariel scrambled for a witty comeback, she heard the front door open and then slam shut. Katie appeared, flung her backpack to the ground in the foyer, and stomped up the stairs to her bedroom. Ariel's heart sank as she realized that her daughter had walked all the way home from school instead of waiting to be picked up.

Miles looked at her, eyes wide.

"I need to go …" Ariel said, giving him an apologetic look. "My daughter."

"I understand. Listen, here's my card." He pulled a small, white business card out of his wallet and handed it to her. On it was his name, number, and a small icon of a majestic sailboat. "I'm only working part-time at the marina, so when you need help here, give me a call."

Ariel walked Miles to the front door, where he gave her a warm, lingering smile before slipping out the door.

Ariel turned and looked back through the foyer and up the stairs, apprehension and worry filling her.

What could have happened at school?

CHAPTER FOURTEEN

Ariel walked up the creaky stairs to Katie's room, her heart heavy with worry. It was only their first night in the house, and already, there was strife.

Katie had chosen the bedroom with the odd door—an old, front door that had been hung in the entrance to the bedroom, looking out of place in the interior of the house. The door was ancient, its surface weathered and scarred from years of exposure to the elements. The rich, dark wood was etched with deep grooves and swirling patterns, testament to the craftsmanship of a bygone era. The brass doorknob was tarnished and worn but still sturdy and functional. A thick, black, iron knocker hung in the center of the door, its shape worn smooth from years of use. The door seemed to radiate a sense of history and mystery, as if it held secrets and stories from long ago. Maybe it knew the secret to making teenaged girls easier to parent.

She knocked on Katie's bedroom door using the old knocker. "Sweetie, can I come in?"

"What do you want?" Katie's voice through the door was cold and distant.

Ariel sighed. "I just wanted to check in with you, see how your day was."

There was a pause before Katie reluctantly responded, "It was fine."

"Just fine?" Ariel asked, trying to keep the conversation going.

"It was terrible, okay?" Katie snapped. Even muffled, Ariel was taken aback by the sharpness in her daughter's voice.

"I hate this new school. I hate this stupid town. I hate everything!"

Ariel kept her voice gentle. "I'm sorry, sweetie. I know it's hard to adjust to a new place. But I promise it'll get better."

Katie let out a bitter laugh. "Yeah, sure. Like how it got better at my old school? When I was getting bullied every day?"

Ariel's heart sank. What else could she have done to defend Katie more strongly from the bullies at her old school? Most of her focus had been on her career and making a name for herself. Was it that she had neglected to be fully present and involved in her daughter's life? She had missed the signs of bullying early on and had not stepped in soon

68

enough to protect Katie from the hurt and pain that she had endured. Ariel now carried the guilt for not being there for her daughter when she needed her the most. But she would make it right and be a better mother from now on. Just as Endless Harbor was supposed to be a fresh start for Ariel, she had hoped the same for Katie.

A terrible thought occurred to Ariel in the ensuing silence. "Oh, Katie, are there problems with bullies here too?"

There was no reply. Acid rose in Ariel's throat. "Why didn't you call me from school?"

"Because I didn't want you to worry," Katie said, her voice softening slightly.

Ariel tried the door handle. It gave easily, and the door swung open. She walked over and sat on the edge of Katie's bed. The girl lay across it, her slender frame curled up under a fluffy pink comforter. Her long, dark hair was splayed out around her, and her eyes were closed tightly as silent tears rolled down her cheeks. Her chest rose and fell with the deep, ragged breaths of someone who was trying to hold back sobs. Her hands were clenched into fists beside her head, and every now and then, she would let out a small, strangled noise that sounded like a cross between a hiccup and a whimper. Her face was blotchy and swollen from crying, and her pillow was damp with tears.

"I'm your mother," Ariel said gently, reaching out to put a hand on Katie's cheek. "It's my job to worry about you. But more importantly, it's my job to protect you. And I'm sorry I didn't do a better job of that at your old school."

There was a long pause before Katie spoke again, opening her eyes a crack. She sniffled. "I just want to be alone right now."

Ariel fought hard not to feel rejected. Instead, she nodded. "Okay, sweetie. But I'm here waiting when you're ready to talk about it. And we *do* need to talk about it. And I'm going to order some burgers and fries. You want some?"

Katie shook her head. "No, I'm not hungry."

Ariel stood up. "Okay, I'll let you be alone. But if you change your mind, just let me know."

As Ariel walked out of the room, she couldn't get out from under the weight of guilt and sadness. She'd thought that the small town would be a place that was safe from the troubles that had plagued them back in Florida. Had she had gotten them all into something that would turn out to be a disaster?

***

As Ariel sat at the dinner table alone, picking at her meal, she relived the day's events—a mixture of good news and bad juju. As a mother, she worried a lot for her daughter. She knew that starting at a new school and adjusting to a new town was never easy, especially after what Katie had gone through at her old school. But she could help Katie, if only Katie would confide in her.

After finishing her dinner, Ariel decided to take a walk along the ocean where she and Miles had determined the new boat slip would go. The salty sea air always seemed to clear her mind and help her think. As she walked, she wracked her brain for memories of her father and the last time she'd seen him. The mystery of his disappearance was always heavy on her mind, something that lingered just outside her conscious thoughts. Had her father worried about them—Ariel, Charlie, their mother? If he was still out there, why had he never come back? What could have been so bad that it had kept him away from his family?

Now that she was a mother, Ariel could never imagine leaving her child.

Worried now about leaving Katie alone when she was upset, Ariel started back toward Leeside. Lost in thought, she didn't realize what she was hearing until a noise pulled her out of her reverie. It sounded like someone was trying to climb the back trellis of her house. With a sense of unease creeping through her, she quickly made her way back to the back yard, her heart pounding in her chest. As she stepped into the moonlit garden, she saw a figure, obscured by the shadows, peering into the window on the back porch. Without hesitation, she ran toward the person, her heart in her throat, determined to find out who it was and what they were doing.

"Hey!" she yelled. "What are you doing on my property?"

But as soon as she got closer, the figure took off, disappearing into the night, leaving her alone and shaken in the darkness.

With her heart still pounding, Ariel scanned the darkness, trying to catch a glimpse of the intruder. But it was as if they had vanished into thin air. She couldn't shake off the unease that now settled in her stomach. Was this just a random act, or was there something more sinister at play? Should she call Charlie and Kurt?

As she mounted the steps and went back into the house, looking fearfully behind her, Ariel couldn't shake the feeling that something was off in the small town of Endless Harbor. She had always thought of it as a safe haven, but now she wasn't so sure.

She would have to be extra vigilant in the days to come.

CHAPTER FIFTEEN

Ariel woke up early the next day, determined to make sure her daughter didn't have another rough day at school. She walked down the hallway to Katie's room and gently knocked on the door.

"Katie, time to wake up," she said softly. But there was no response. Ariel opened the door to find Katie still fast asleep, wrapped tightly in her blankets.

Ariel stopped to take in the room. Katie's bedroom was the first they had cleaned out, and it was located in the turret of the old Victorian house. The room had a lot of architectural charm, but it was also quite shabby. The walls were painted a pale yellow, but the paint was chipped and peeling in several places. The hardwood floors were scuffed and in need of a good sanding and staining. The room was circular, with a high ceiling and a large window that looked out over the neighborhood. The window was adorned with a set of heavy drapes that were frayed and discolored from age.

In the center of the room stood a four-poster bed, which was made of dark, polished wood and had a thick, ornate headboard. The bed was dressed in a frilly, white canopy and matching bedspread that looked like they were from another era. The bed was comfortable, but even with a new mattress, it sagged in the middle and the box spring creaked with every movement. The room was dimly lit by a small table lamp that sat on the bedside table, casting a warm, golden glow over the room. Despite the shabby condition, the room had a certain charm that made it feel cozy and inviting.

Ariel shook her gently, "Come on, sweetie, you don't want to be late."

Katie groaned and rolled over. "I don't want to go," she mumbled.

Ariel sat down on the edge of the bed and stroked her daughter's hair. "I have an idea. Why don't we go out for breakfast? My treat."

Ariel could tell that Katie was still feeling upset from the previous day's events, and it made her heart ache to see her daughter so down.

"Come on, sweetie, let's get you up," Ariel said, trying to sound cheerful. "I'll take you out for breakfast. How does that sound?"

Katie grumbled something unintelligible and rolled over, pulling the covers over her head. Ariel sighed and sat down on the edge of the bed. "You have to go to school. You can't let them get to you."

Her own turn of phrase sent a chill up Ariel's spine. She thought about the mysterious figure the previous night, and how spooked she had felt. Who had it been, and had they been trying to get to Katie and Ariel?

After some persuasion, Ariel managed to get Katie out of bed and into the car. They drove to the Throwback Diner in town, where they ordered blueberry waffles. As they waited for their food, Ariel could see the sadness in her daughter's eyes.

"What's wrong, Katie?" Ariel asked, reaching across the table to take her daughter's hand. "And don't just tell me nothing. I can't help you if I'm in the dark."

Katie shook her head, looking away. Ariel refused to let her sit in silence.

Ariel forged on. "How was your first day at school?"

The waitress—Jill, again, who smiled at them both but slipped quietly away as though she sensed the tension at the table—arrived with their plates, and Ariel sat, not touching hers, staring at her daughter.

"Terrible," Katie grumbled, pushing her waffles around her plate with her fork.

"What happened?" Ariel asked, concern etched on her face.

"Everyone was so different from what I'm used to," Katie said, her voice barely above a whisper. "It's just ... the kids at this school, they made fun of me for being from Miami. They said I talk funny and that I don't belong here if I'm not from here."

Ariel wanted nothing more than to wave a magic wand and fix everything for Katie. She knew how hard it was to be the new kid in school. It had happened to her when she'd left Endless Harbor for college. But she had been older and better able to cope with the change. "I'm so sorry, sweetie. That's not fair. But you know what? I don't fit in here either. Not yet at least. I'm not sure I even used to when I was your age."

"But why can't I fit in anywhere?" Katie asked, her voice small and defeated. "I know I said I was happy in Miami, but I wasn't."

Ariel took her daughter's hand. "I don't know. But it's too early to tell. And Miami ended up sucking for me too. Why don't we make a deal? If we don't like it here by the end of the school year, we'll go somewhere else, *and* I'll homeschool you."

Katie looked up at her mother, her eyes filled with hope. "Really?"

"Of course," Ariel said with a smile. "We're in this together, no matter what."

Ariel left her own doubts unsaid—with the obstacles in her way with the mayor, and now the mysterious figure lurking around Leeside, Ariel herself was beginning to feel like they should cut bait and run from her childhood home.

CHAPTER SIXTEEN

As soon as Katie was off to school, Ariel was back to work at Leeside. Ariel and Charlene were working together in the living room of the old Victorian house, surrounded by paint cans and tools. Ariel stood back and surveyed the living room, hoping they would submit to restoration. The walls were a dingy white, but they had been well patched where they'd cracked, and once painted, Ariel had big plans for this space. She had purchased several gallons of paint in a pale blue color and was ready to get to work.

As she began to paint, excitement swirled through her. This was the next step in transforming this run-down house into a beautiful bed and breakfast. The paint went on smoothly, and she took care to cover every inch of the walls.

While she worked, Ariel's mind wandered. She thought about her plans for the house and the challenges she would face in making it a reality. She thought about the pushback from the mayor and the possibility of the rebel group in the tight-knit community of Endless Harbor. Was Miles part of the rebel group? He had had his own tussle with trying to establish a business in town.

Ariel carefully rolled paint onto the walls of the living room, her sister Charlene by her side, working on the other half of the room. Ariel loved that the two of them had been working on the house together, slowly bringing it back to life. The living room was already starting to look like a completely different room. The once-dingy walls were now a soft, pale blue, and the woodwork was crisp and white.

Ariel paused for a moment to admire their work, a sense of accomplishment washing over her. "I can't believe we're actually doing this," she said, smiling at Charlene.

"I know, right?" Charlene replied. "It's hard work, but it's so satisfying to see the progress we're making."

Ariel nodded in agreement, her gaze scanning the room. "We still have a long way to go, but I can see the potential here. This place is going to be beautiful when we're done with it."

Charlene grinned. "And it's all thanks to you, sis. You're the one with the vision, I'm just here to help."

"I couldn't have done it without you," Ariel said, grateful for her sister's support. "I'm just glad you're here to share this with me."

Charlene seemed to pause on the way to speaking. Then she said, "I doubted you, Ari. Heck, I still have some doubts. But I see how determined you are, and so I promise to help you see this through."

Ariel felt her mouth go dry and her eyes grow wet. "Thanks, sis." She started to tell Charlie about the mysterious figure, but the thought of ruining her sister's sudden strong support gave Ariel pause. She would find a way to tell Charlie—later.

The two of them worked in companionable silence for a while longer, the sound of the paint rollers and the occasional scrape of a ladder the only noise in the room. As the light started to fade, Ariel stepped back again to admire her handiwork. The pale blue walls brought a freshness to the room, and she could already imagine the furniture and decor that would fill the space. She was pleased with the progress she had made and couldn't wait to tackle the next project.

Charlene went into the kitchen and returned with two mugs of tea and a plate filled with crackers and cheese. Ariel sat with her sister at a makeshift table they'd set up at the back of the living room. It was made of scrap plywood set across sawhorses, and she had been thrilled at their inventiveness.

"Oh my gosh, Charlene, I just know this is going to be amazing," Ariel exclaimed, her eyes sparkling with excitement. "I have so many ideas for decorating the guest rooms and creating menus for the guests."

"I can't wait to see it all come together," Charlene said, smiling. "And I have a few ideas for the garden too. We should definitely incorporate some local flowers and plants. You know, you could even set up a little shop, sell the produce and the flowers. I could get you that hand cream from my old company—"

Ariel cut her eyes over at Charlie. "Char, if you bring one tube of that MLM lotion near my B&B ..."

"How about a wraparound porch with rocking chairs, and a fire pit out back for s'mores?" Charlie said, quickly changing the subject.

"That sounds lovely," Ariel said, laughing. "And I love all of these ideas. But there's the cost. Of course, I have thought about that. I've got a budget and everything."

Charlie sipped her tea, and Ariel followed suit, taking a deep breath and turning toward her sister. "In fact, I have a bit of a surprise—the house in Miami sold just this morning."

Charlie set her teacup down and squealed. "What? Really?"

Ariel grinned. "For over asking price! I've been going over all the forms and permits I'll need to fight the mayor's blockade, and I even feel better about that. It seems doable. I was feeling so down about everything, but now—I see a way through."

"I can *see* that," Charlene said with a chuckle. "You're just like Dad, always so determined."

"Yeah, well, someone's got to be," Ariel said, her smile faltering for a moment at the mention of their missing father.

"Hey," Charlene said, noticing her sister's change in demeanor, "it's going to be okay. We'll get this place fixed up and the B&B running in no time. And who knows? Maybe the mayor will come around. Your plans will knock his socks off."

"Yeah, maybe he will."

Ariel knew it was the right time to bring up the strange occurrences that had been happening around the property. She set her own mug down and leaned in toward Charlie.

"I have to tell you something else," she started.

Charlie set her own mug down, her expression curious.

"I keep seeing people lurking around the house like they're checking it out or something," Ariel said, furrowing her brow in concern. "First, it was this old woman—she said her name was Doris, and she seemed to know Dad. And then, last night, someone was looking in the back window. I didn't see who it was. They ran off."

Charlene shrugged. "Doris is certifiable. She's been here about ten years, bought the parcel next to Leeside, the land with the little cottage on it. I bet she and Dad talked, makes sense if they were neighbors. But she's harmless."

"And the window-peeker?" Ariel asked.

"That's probably just developers looking to buy the place. They sneak on to get the lay of the land because most folks here want to keep what they have. I mean, some were swayed by high price offers, but if the developers can find something on your land that's of public benefit, I wouldn't put it past Stanton to try to grab this place up under some byzantine eminent domain law."

But Ariel wasn't satisfied with her sister's explanation. "It's just strange, like someone is watching me or something," she said, looking down at the teacup in her hand.

"But I just thought you should know." To lighten the suddenly heavy vibe in the room, Ariel chirped, "I did get some help with the building projects. In fact, Miles Clemens is coming by tomorrow to help me reframe the stair railing." Ariel tried her best to play it cool as she dropped the detail on her sister.

Charlene's eyes widened in surprise. "Really? You know, you never told me. How did you meet the mysterious man of the marina?"

Ariel laughed, trying to downplay the situation—the situation being that Miles Clemens was pretty nice to look at, and he would be here at her house for quite some time, regularly. "Oh, just at the marina. Then he came by. He offered to help me out with some of the work here in exchange for access to our bit of shoreline."

Charlene nodded, but her expression turned serious. "Miles is a bit of a mystery around here. He keeps to himself, so he fits in well in Endless Harbor. But there's talk that he's some former corporate bigwig who came here after he cheated on his wife."

Ariel's face fell in shock. "What? That can't be true. He seemed so nice and helpful. Not at all like some soap-opera villain."

Charlene shrugged. "I don't know if it's true or not. But it's best to be cautious around here. People aren't always who they seem."

Ariel felt uneasy. Maybe there was more to Miles than she initially thought. She certainly didn't have room in her life for another unfaithful man—and could she even be friends with someone who'd cheated on his spouse? The sour feeling that she'd felt when she'd discovered Dylan's betrayal churned in her stomach.

As Charlene stood up from the table, she stretched her arms above her head, a groan of discomfort escaping her lips. "Well, I hate to break up the fun, but I've got to get going," she said, grabbing her purse from the nearby chair. "I've got a Spoiled Pet Products party to host in an hour."

Ariel raised an eyebrow playfully. "Another MLM? You're becoming quite the social butterfly," she teased. "Don't give them my phone number."

Charlene rolled her eyes good-naturedly. "Hey, a girl's got to make a living," she said with a grin.

Ariel stood up as well, giving her sister a hug. "Thanks for all your help today. I couldn't have done this without you."

"Anytime, honey," Charlene said, returning the hug. "I'll see you in a couple days at the presentation."

With one last wave, Charlene made her way to the door and stepped out, leaving Ariel alone. Katie would be home soon, and Ariel would need to be ready for whatever her day had brought on.

CHAPTER SEVENTEEN

The next few days went by in a blur. Katie had come home after Ariel and Charlie's painting day without much to report—and since the first day, she hadn't had any more incidents at school. But her enthusiasm for Endless Harbor didn't grow, either. Ariel was left over the course of several nights to think about her promise to Katie—happiness or the highway. Where else would they go? Could Ariel find work in some other city, maybe back in the kitchen of a fine restaurant? Back in Paris, at the Frogmore—the five-star steakhouse where she had realized some of her greatest ideas to fruition—Ariel remembered being so happy there.

But for now, Ariel stood in front of the mirror, smoothing down her blazer and straightening her skirt. She was nervous but determined.

She had put together all of the proper forms and filings for the board meeting that evening, where she would make her case for the city openly allowing her to run a bed and breakfast in Endless Harbor. She knew it wouldn't be easy, but nothing since Miami had been.

As she walked to the community center where the meeting was being held, she tried to push aside her sense of unease. The streets were quiet, and the community center was mostly empty. She was relieved when she saw Charlene, Kurt, Peter, and Hannah waiting for her outside. They had come to support her. Katie lurked behind the others, looking sulky.

"Thanks for coming," Ariel said, giving her sister a hug.

"Of course," Charlene said, smiling. "We're here for you."

Ariel wrapped her arms tightly around Katie as soon as she could reach her, noticing the sullen look on her daughter's face. She could feel the tension in Katie's body as she hugged her back, and Ariel knew that something was troubling her.

"What's wrong, sweetheart?" Ariel asked softly, rubbing her daughter's back in a soothing manner. "Did something happen at school?"

"No," Katie said. "I'm just tired."

Ariel had to let it slide for now, though she would be talking with Katie tonight. She squared her shoulders and walked into the community center, feeling a little more at ease with her family by her side.

The community center was a large, plain room with white walls and a linoleum floor. At the front of the room was a long, wooden table, behind which sat the board members and the mayor. They were all dressed in suits and looked serious as they perused their papers. In front of them were rows of chairs, set up for the community members to address the board. A microphone stood on a podium in the center aisle between the chairs, waiting for the first speaker to step up. Ariel felt her heart pounding as she marched her way to the front of the room. She could feel the weighted gazes of the room as she stepped up to the microphone. Ariel took a deep breath and mentally rehearsed her presentation, hoping that her proposal for her bed and breakfast would be met with favor from the board.

There was no doubt that this was going to be an uphill battle. Ariel fixed the front of the room with her gaze, and her eyes fell squarely on Mayor Stanton—the nemesis that she had not even met in person yet.

The man was tall—she could tell that even though he was seated. He had the look of a retired boxer—balding, with a bullish, square face and a heavy brow. His suit was tailored across his broad shoulders in a way that Ariel thought was probably meant to highlight how physically intimidating he was.

So, this is who I'm up against?

The mayor had made it clear from the start that he was against Ariel's plans for the bed and breakfast, and she could see the disdain in his dark eyes as she began her presentation.

"Good evening," Ariel began, her voice shaking slightly. "I am here to propose a bed and breakfast at Leeside, the historic Victorian house on Ocean Boulevard. This house has been in my family for generations, and I believe it has the potential to be a valuable asset to the community."

The mayor interrupted her, "I'm afraid I must disagree. This town has bigger plans for Ocean Boulevard, plans that don't include a small, run-down bed and breakfast."

Ariel pressed on, "But I believe that my bed and breakfast will bring much-needed revenue to the town."

A murmur went up from the small crowd behind her. Ariel suspected that not too many people spoke back when Stanton talked.

The mayor scoffed. "You're wasting our time with this pipe dream. The board has better things to do than listen to this nonsense." He looked around for support, and Ariel saw surprise cross his features when no one immediately spoke up.

One of the board members—a younger man in a crisp suit and tie—did speak up. "I, for one, would like to hear her out. I believe it's important to consider all options for the future of our town."

The mayor grumbled but relented, and Ariel continued her presentation. She highlighted the potential for jobs and economic growth, as well as the unique charm of the Victorian house. The board members listened attentively, and Ariel could sense a shift in the room.

As Ariel continued to present her case to the board, she could feel the eyes of the mayor on her, boring into her with a mixture of annoyance and disdain. He kept interrupting her, trying to shut her down and dismiss her ideas before she had even finished speaking. She pulled out her permit forms and read off all the ones that she had prepared, but he bombarded her with questions about more that she had "failed to file."

Just as Ariel was about to lose hope, a middle-aged woman whose name badge said "Susan" spoke up in her defense.

"Mayor Stanton, I think it's only fair that we hear her out and review all the facts before making a decision," Susan said firmly, her voice carrying across the room.

"Fine," he said through gritted teeth.

Ariel tried to steady her nerves. She knew she had to make a strong last argument if she wanted her dream to become a reality. "I understand your concerns, but I believe that my business will not only create jobs and boost the economy, but it will also preserve the historical charm of our town. You can see how so much of Endless Harbor is going away—yes, the new marina is nice, and yes, the resort that's planned will be nice too. But I remember a different town from my childhood. One where all the old houses were lovingly cared for, where the fishermen and the tourists didn't live in two different towns. I want people to be able to come here and see what I saw in this place when I was a child. And I don't think you can fully do that from the deck of a million-dollar yacht, or from a sterile, glass-and-steel resort."

The mayor scoffed, but Susan nodded in agreement, her eyes warm. "I agree, Ariel. We should at least consider all options before making a decision."

"But the town already has enough small businesses," the mayor argued. "We need to focus on bigger developments like the resort I have planned. The tax implications—"

Ariel stood her ground. "With all due respect, Mr. Mayor, your proposed resort may bring in more money, but it also runs the risk of losing the small-town charm that makes Endless Harbor unique, the very charm that comes from its everyday citizens, who will keep your *tax base* alive when the snow sets in and the season passes for day sailing and mimosas in the pool. Leeside will provide an alternative that appeals to a different kind of tourist, one who values the authenticity of a small community."

Some of the board members nodded in agreement.

"Fine," the Mayor said again. Ariel was beginning to think that it was the only word he might be capable of in his frustration. "We can table this for discussion at a later time, then."

Ariel felt a thrill of temporary victory, but she knew it was not over yet. The mayor would come with big guns next time. He was only giving himself more time to come back against her.

"Provisional approval granted," Susan said, and a gavel was pounded.

As they walked out of the community center, Charlene and Kurt were all smiles, high fiving each other and congratulating Ariel on a job well done. "We won, sis! You really showed that mayor who's boss," Charlene exclaimed, her voice filled with excitement.

Katie, however, was less enthused. "But we didn't win yet, right Mom?" she asked, looking up at Ariel with a concerned expression.

Ariel shook her head. "No, not yet. The vote was tabled, and we have provisional approval, which means they'll review the facts and make a final decision at the next meeting. And I'm sure the mayor will bring in some heavy hitters to try and sway the vote in his favor," she said, her voice tinged with a hint of worry.

Kurt, sensing the shift in the mood, put a hand on Ariel's shoulder. "But you did great, and we'll be there to support you every step of the way."

Ariel smiled, grateful for her brother-in-law's support. "Thanks, Kurt. I just hope it's enough."

CHAPTER EIGHTEEN

The seafood restaurant where they all landed for dinner that night was alive with the sound of laughter and chatter as Ariel, Charlene, Kurt, and all the kids sat on the back deck, huddled around a small table, strategizing against the mayor. The air was chilly, but there was a sweetness in it that hinted at the approaching April, and the group was bundled up in warm jackets, their hands wrapped around steaming cups of hot cocoa.

"We need to gather more support," Ariel said, her eyes scanning the group as they discussed their plan of action.

"I can put up flyers around town," Charlene offered. "And I can talk to some of the local business owners, see if they'll back us."

Ariel remembered what Bob had said about the rebels in town, folks starting to unite against the resort—it couldn't be that Charlie and Kurt were part of that, could it?

"I'll reach out to some of the other marina owners," Kurt added. "They're not going to be happy about the Mayor's plan for a spa resort either."

Interesting, Ariel thought.

Ariel passed around plates of lobster and corn, meals that everyone had ordered at the urging of Charlene and Kurt.

Peter and Hannah excitedly picked at their food, trying to crack open their lobster. Katie, who had never had lobster before, tentatively picked at hers. She had never tried lobster before, but at her mother's urging, she tentatively took a bite. Her eyes widened in delight as the flavors burst in her mouth.

"Wow," she exclaimed, taking another bite. "This is so good!"

The group laughed, happy to have a moment of levity amidst their serious planning.

"Glad you like it, sweetie. It's a New England classic," Charlene said, reaching over to ruffle Katie's hair. "Maybe we'll make this a tradition, celebrating our victories with a seafood feast."

"Victories yet to come," Ariel corrected, her determination clear in her voice. "We haven't won yet, but we will."

As they continued to discuss and plan, the group chatted, the air filled with excitement and optimism for the future. They would fight for their right to open a B&B in Endless Harbor, and they would win.

When their meal was finished and the last plate cleared away, and after they had all declined dessert with groans of being too full, they left the restaurant and began to walk.

As the sun began to set, Peter and Hannah excitedly dragged Katie and Ariel down to the harbor to see the boats. Ariel took in the sights and sounds of the marina, feeling a sense of belonging she had not felt since moving to Endless Harbor.

The marina was eerily quiet as evening approached, the only sounds coming from the gentle lapping of the water against the dock and the distant hum of a passing car. The boats bobbed gently in their slips, their masts casting long shadows across the water. The air was cool and salty, carrying with it the scent of the sea. The only light came from the pale moon and the occasional streetlamp, casting a soft glow over the scene. The dock creaked as a figure made their way down the wooden planks, their footsteps echoing in the stillness. The only sign of life was the gentle swaying of ropes and the occasional flapping of a sail. It was a peaceful, serene scene, but also a little eerie in the dark. Ariel thought of the figure who'd been lurking around the house, and she turned away from the boat slips.

As they walked along the dock, Charlene and Kurt joined them, and they all chatted about their plans for the future.

"It's so beautiful here," Ariel said, taking in the sights of the boats bobbing on the water.

"It's a shame the mayor wants to change all of that," Charlene said, her tone tinged with sadness. "He's been trying to push out the small businesses and change the town's identity to attract more tourists. But he won't let you open up when that would attract them too. It stinks like week-old fish."

"We won't let him win," Ariel said, feeling a knot form in her stomach as she thought about her own plans for a bed and breakfast.

"Endless Harbor has always been a place for the local community," Kurt added. "But the mayor seems to want to take that away. He's been buying up all this land and pushing out people who have lived here for generations."

Ariel listened to her sister and brother-in-law, feeling a sense of determination growing within her. She was not going to let the mayor take away the history and charm of this town. She would see her dreams realized—and the dreams of the community.

Ariel felt a burning anger in her chest as Charlene and Kurt spoke about the mayor's plans. She couldn't believe that someone would try to take away the history of the town her mother and father had loved so much. She could almost hear her dad's voice in her head, urging her to push toward what she believed in, just like he would have. She knew that if he were still here, he would have been standing right next to her, fighting for her bed and breakfast alongside her.

Don't let them get you down, Ari. They're ordinary. You are extraordinary.

She was determined to honor his memory by standing up against the mayor and fighting for her dreams, no matter how hard it may be.

***

Katie came running back up the shore to where the adults stood, looking distraught.

Ariel's chest tightened as she saw the tears streaming down Katie's face. "What's wrong, sweetie?" she asked, pulling her daughter into a hug.

"Those mean kids," Katie sniffled. "The ones from school who were calling me names and saying I don't belong here."

"Who are they?" Ariel asked, her anger growing.

"Peter and Hannah said they were some kids from their neighborhood," Katie replied, wiping at her eyes. "That boy—the one from the harbor the first night we were here—he's with them. He goes to school with me."

"Honey, is he one of the ones who made fun of how you talk that first day at school?"

Katie choked back a sob. "I'm going to the car." And then she was off down the sidewalk, leaving Ariel staring after. Peter and Hannah jogged up, worry on their faces as they watched Katie go.

Ariel turned to Charlene and Kurt, her eyes filled with fury. "Those must be the same kids who have been bullying Katie at school," she exclaimed. "I can't believe they would do this to her, here, of all places."

"I'm so sorry, Ariel," Charlene said, looking ashamed. "I had no idea any local kids would do something like this. I'm sure we can find out who their parents are. We'll talk to them, I promise."

"No, *I'll* talk to them," Ariel said determinedly. "I'm not going to let them bully my daughter, or anyone else for that matter. I don't care if we have been gone—this is still my town."

Ariel seethed with rage as she flashed back to the times that she failed to help Katie when bullies tormented her at her old school. They all walked to the car in tense silence, and Charlie hugged Ariel before the two families went their separate ways.

Now, Ariel was determined to protect Katie from the *new* bullies. She felt a mother's ferocity, ready to do battle. With her fists clenched, and anger rising within her like a boiling current, she was ready to unleash its fury.

CHAPTER NINETEEN

The silence on the ride home was heavy.

Ariel and Katie had been in the car for nearly fifteen minutes before Katie finally started to explain why the boy from the harbor was picking on her.

"He said," she began, her voice small and hesitant, "that he knows something about you, Mom. That it's why he's been picking on me."

Ariel felt a chill run up her spine, and she glanced over at her daughter, trying to hide her fear. She knew what Katie was talking about—the fight with the mayor and maybe whoever the developers he'd been working with who had been trying to block their business. But what did some teenage boy have to do with that? Had this boy been the one who'd been lurking around the house?

"What did he say?" Ariel asked, hoping that it wasn't anything too serious.

Katie shrugged. "He just said he knows you're going to have to leave town soon. And we should go back to Miami. He's really mad at me for *some* reason. And that it's why he's been picking on me. And there's one other thing. He—" Katie's voice went soft. "The mayor is his dad. His name is Connor Stanton."

Ariel felt her heart sink. She had been afraid that something like this might happen. She'd been through corporate negotiations that were high-pressure and nerve-wracking, but she felt lost as to what to do to navigate the strange, small-town war she was fighting. She had thought that she could protect her daughter from all of this, but it seemed that she had failed. She wished she had done more, but it was too late now. There were more battles than she'd expected.

"What should I do?" Ariel asked, her voice barely a whisper. "I want to go mama bear on everyone I can find who is involved, but I also want you to decide. Do you want me to go talk to the school?"

Katie seemed to consider this for a moment before she finally spoke. "No. I think," she said slowly, "that you should talk to the mayor."

Ariel closed her eyes. She knew that it was probably the right thing to do, but she also wasn't sure if she was ready to face the father of the boy who had been picking on her daughter. Especially since he was also her enemy. And he'd avoided her before—his blonde secretary might as well have been a brick wall.

"I don't know if I can," she said.

Katie reached out and squeezed her mother's hand. "Please? For me?" she said softly. "Maybe you can work out the bullying and find a way for the resort and our B&B to stay."

Ariel nodded. She knew that her daughter was right. She had to face this head-on, no matter how afraid she felt. And had Katie just said *our B&B*?

"Okay," Ariel said, taking a deep breath. "I'll talk to him."

Katie smiled, and Ariel felt a surge of love for her daughter. No matter how difficult things got, she could always rely on her to be brave and wise.

"Thank you, Mom," Katie said.

Ariel returned her daughter's smile. "Thank you, too," she said, and they drove the rest of the way home in silence.

***

Once they were home and Katie had gone off to bed, Ariel tried to relax. She took a stack of home design magazines and settled on the worn sofa in the living room. She hadn't been settled for more than ten minutes when she heard the doorbell ring. She quickly made her way to answer it.

When she opened the door, she was greeted by Miles, who had a look of concern on his face. "Is everything okay?" he asked. "How did the board meeting go? Was the mayor his old, welcoming self?"

"Oh, it's just a little neighborhood drama," Ariel replied, trying to play it off as nothing.

"One of my marina employees was down at the shore helping a customer. I heard some kids were giving Katie a hard time," Miles said, his voice firm. "I would have come to find you, but I didn't want to interrupt if your family was with you. And I didn't want to overstep."

Ariel thought about how Charlene would have reacted if Miles had shown up. Ariel herself was unsure of the rumors swirling about the handsome man.

"Yeah, some new bullies at her school," Ariel said, her own voice growing angrier. "But we're handling it."

"If there's anything I can do to help, just let me know," Miles offered, shifting from foot to foot on the porch.

"Thanks, Miles," Ariel said, her anger and uncertainty dissipating a bit at his kind offer. "And actually, the board meeting went okay. They tabled the vote, so I have to come back with more information."

"That's not a defeat," Miles said, trying to be positive. "It's just a delay. And I know you'll come back stronger."

"Thanks, Miles," Ariel said, giving him a small smile. "I appreciate the support."

"Anytime," Miles said. Then, after a pause, he said, "Well, I'd better …"

"Oh! Would you like to come in?"

He nodded and smiled, and Ariel stepped to the side to let him in.

"I've got some tea," she offered, leading him into the kitchen. "It's not fancy or anything, but it's warm and relaxing."

He followed Ariel into the kitchen, where she set about making tea for the both of them.

Miles took a seat at the kitchen table. "Tea sounds perfect, actually," he said.

Ariel busied herself with the teapot and mugs while Miles looked around, admiring the cozy atmosphere of her home. "You're getting some real work done here," he said.

"Thanks to help from Charlene and you."

"So, what brings you all the way up here?" Ariel asked, not wanting to seem intrusive. "You said you aren't originally from this area?"

"I needed a fresh start," Miles replied casually, echoing his last answer. "And I had to go where the boats were." He didn't give any more details though, so Ariel dropped it and continued making tea in silence. It was obvious that there was a lot more to him than what she saw on the surface. He wasn't wearing a wedding ring. Did he leave his wife because of an affair? Was that why he seemed so guarded?

Eventually she set a mug in front of him along with some cream and the sugar bowl beside it. She sat down across from him with her own mug of steaming tea, and they both sipped quietly for a few moments before Miles spoke again.

"This was very kind of you," he said softly with a slight smile on his face. "Thank you."

Ariel smiled back at him, suddenly overcome by emotion as she realized how much she enjoyed spending time with this mysterious man who had come into her life unexpectedly yet seemed like an old friend already. She wanted to ask him more questions—about his family, why he moved here, even about the possibility of his ex-wife—but something told her that now was not the right time to pry further into his life story like that. So instead, they continued drinking their tea together in pleasant silence.

Ariel was intrigued by Miles, despite herself. After all, she had just been through a bad break up with Dylan who cheated on her. She felt like maybe this could be a good thing for her—a chance to start anew. But there were still many unanswered questions and much left unsaid between them.

Miles cleared his throat, breaking the silence. "I want you to know that I'm not just here for tea," he said with a shy smile. "My hobby is restoring old boats—just like you're restoring this old house."

Ariel was surprised by his admission and delightedly smiled back at him. She couldn't believe how much they already had in common. And that he was offering this information unprompted.

"That's amazing!" she exclaimed. "How in the world does someone pick boat restoration as a hobby?"

Miles looked down into his mug of tea and seemed to be gathering his thoughts before speaking again. "Well, you know how many people enjoy working on cars?" he asked rhetorically. "It's kind of the same thing with boats—except there are no spark plugs or oil filters. It all comes down to sanding the hull, varnishing the wood, replacing rotten planks—all that kind of stuff." He paused for a moment and then continued with a smile. "It's really quite therapeutic and calming, kind of like what you're doing here with your house restoration project. I come out with a boat that looks brand new but with all its original character still intact." He sighed contentedly as though lost in his own thoughts for a moment before adding, "And I think it's important to remember our pasts sometimes even if they weren't pleasant—so we can appreciate how far we've come."

Ariel stared at Miles in fascination as he spoke and found herself drawn to him even more than before—such passion and dedication toward something so intricate was remarkable and inspiring. After all, restoring an old boat or an old house wasn't just about fixing up something broken but also finding beauty in its history and making it new again. His words struck a chord in Ariel. She appreciated that Miles saw what she was doing in the house, since only her family so far understood why she was working so hard to make it beautiful again.

"That's really cool," she said, smiling up at him. "It must be so satisfying to take something old and bring it back to life."

Ariel thought she saw a hint of sadness pass over his face but didn't want to pry any further. They lapsed again into silence.

90

After a few more minutes, Miles set his mug down and cleared his throat. "Well, I should probably be heading out," he said regretfully.

Ariel nodded in understanding and stood up to walk him to the door. As they got there, Miles turned around and smiled at her warmly. "Thank you for the tea—and for listening to me ramble on about old boats," he said with a chuckle.

"It was no problem at all," Ariel replied sincerely as she opened the door for him. "And now that the stair railings look so nice, maybe we can start on the porch? Whenever you're free."

Miles looked surprised but pleased by her invitation, then nodded in agreement. He held out a hand to shake, but instead, she said her goodbye with a spontaneous hug. He stiffened in her arms, but then he seemed to relax against her. His eyes were warm when they parted.

She watched him walk away with a pang of regret that their time together had ended so soon. He waved goodbye one last time before disappearing into the darkness that enveloped the driveway, leaving Ariel alone with her thoughts.

CHAPTER TWENTY

The next day, Ariel decided it was time for her to go meet with Mayor Stanton. She had promised Katie she would step in and get her out of her current situation with the school bullies *without* involving the school.

As she drove into Endless Harbor's downtown, Ariel felt a chill of apprehension ripple through her body. She wasn't sure what sort of reception she would get from the mayor, and she hoped it wasn't anything too unpleasant. Sure, they were at odds over the B&B, but he couldn't be that bad—though, deep down, she suspected that he wouldn't be as pleasant as Miles had been. Her face heated at the memory of their farewell hug the previous night.

She parked by the mayor's office. Ariel told herself not to be intimated. She recalled him from the last board meeting, remembering how nervous she had been then. He'd had a slimy demeanor about him, his almost-absent hair slicked back in a wispy combover, and his suit had looked like it was straight out of a gangster movie.

When she arrived, she stood for a moment admiring the tall pillars that lined the exterior of the building, the huge windows that allowed natural light to flood into the open space within, and even more intricate designs carved onto each window's frame. The entrance was surrounded by an array of flower beds that would add an extra touch of charm to this place in warmer weather.

Upon entering the mayor's office itself—surprisingly easy, and even with the blessing of the icy blonde—Ariel found herself standing in an enormous chamber that could easily fit ten people inside it. The walls were lined with shelves filled with books seemingly written in all different languages. There was a mahogany desk sitting directly in front of an enormous window which allowed natural light to stream in and brighten up the entire room. Several chairs were placed around it for visitors or guests. A large conference table sat off to one side where important meetings took place. Even the carpet beneath her feet was soft and luxurious looking.

The mayor waved her into his office without a word, motioning for her to take a seat across from him. Ariel nodded and accepted his invitation, taking in everything around her—from marble statues on either side of doorways to crystal chandeliers illuminating gilded walls that were adorned with awards and diplomas presented by city leaders spanning generations before them; it seemed almost like an art gallery rather than a workplace!

Ariel sank into the chair, her expression determined. "I need your help," she began. "Your son seems to be giving my daughter some trouble at school."

The mayor cleared his throat and waved a dismissive hand. "My son isn't a bully," he said. "He is a bit of an alpha male and may have come off as intimidating to your daughter, but I can assure you that he never means any harm. Probably more of a misunderstanding than anything else. I'm sure there is some other explanation for your daughter's problems at school. Maybe the stress of the renovations you are doing at home?" He looked up from his desk, fixing her with a haughty stare. "You should take a step back and focus on helping her, instead."

Ariel sat back in her chair, incredulous at the suggestion. "That's not going to solve this problem," she said firmly. She tried to keep her voice level and calm despite her anger bubbling inside of her. "I need you to take concrete steps to stop the bullying, or else I'm going to have to take matters into my own hands, like going on social media and publicly outing your stance on bullying."

The mayor raised his eyebrows in surprise and shock at Ariel's words. Clearly, he had not expected this kind of response from her. He grunted, annoyance clouding his face. He quickly recovered though, leaning forward with a serious expression on his face as he replied. "Now hold up there—I don't think that's necessary," he said slowly, carefully choosing each word as if testing how far she was willing to go. "We can handle this situation without involving anyone outside of this office."

He softened his voice as he added, "Please believe me when I say that I am genuinely concerned about all of this and want what's best for all involved here."

Ariel seriously suspected that he had just used his politician's voice on her, and she didn't find it nearly as effective as her or Charlene's mom voice.

The mayor leaned back in his chair and flashed her a smooth smile. "I'd be more than happy to come up with a solution. Maybe over dinner or drinks sometime soon. You are welcome to bring your husband."

Ariel bristled, her fingers gripping the armrest of her chair in an ironclad hold. Keeping her voice even, she replied, "I'm not married."

"Oh," he said, his eyes lighting up. "Just the two of us, then?"

She caught his drift, and she didn't particularly like it. "I'm afraid that's not possible. We can solve this here." She sat up straighter in her chair and got out her phone, as if to record. "Now let's get back to the business at hand—this needs to be resolved as quickly and efficiently as possible."

The mayor eyed her carefully before nodding his head in agreement. "You're right, of course. I'll make sure all parties involved receive a proper talking to, and we can move on from this incident as soon as possible."

He stared at her until she tucked her phone away—his silence a clear message.

I'm not going to say anything you can catch me at.

Ariel gave him a curt nod before standing up abruptly and exiting the office, her heels clicking on the expensive flooring.

Even though, she'd had to resort to threatening bad publicity, Ariel was relieved that the mayor seemed to be actually taking her seriously this time.

But her relief was soon replaced by fear and anxiety. She knew that even if the mayor did follow through on his promise and took care of this situation, there would still be the possibility that the teens ignored him. Being a single mother was difficult enough without having to worry about Katie's safety while at school. Ariel knew the incident with Katie's bullies was only a small part of the problem; deep down, Ariel feared that she wasn't enough for Katie as a mom, that she couldn't protect her daughter against all the meanness of the world.

People had let her down before—first her ex-husband who had left them without so much as a backward glance and then Dylan with Mitzi, the replacement girlfriend.

As she walked away, Ariel felt the pressure of being a single mother just trying to do right by her daughter but not quite managing it. She fought back tears as she made her way out onto the street. The thought of being alone in all this made Ariel's stomach churn, and for a moment, she felt like giving up altogether. What could she really do against powerful figures like Stanton?

But then she thought of her daughter, who needed someone to fight for her, and if nobody else would do it, then Ariel was determined to take on that role herself. And she wasn't alone. She had Charlie, Kurt, and even Miles.

94

With newfound resolve, she straightened her shoulders and pulled out her phone to check the time. She still had a few hours before she had to meet Katie after school. The sun was high and warm, and she couldn't sit in the house alone with her own thoughts, so instead of heading home right away, Ariel decided to go get lunch at the diner. Maybe some comfort food would help lift her spirits, at least temporarily until this whole bullying situation was finally resolved once and for all.

CHAPTER TWENTY ONE

Ariel decided to take a detour on her way to lunch, walking past the harbor and its boats bobbing peacefully in the water. It was a beautiful day, and the sun's rays glimmered off of the waves, which lapped gently against each other—a reminder of how life could be so peaceful at times. It felt surreal to be here in this moment, as if everything else was forgotten while she just enjoyed soaking up the beauty of this place.

Ariel made her way through the town, nodding at familiar faces as she went. She was beginning to recognize locals, and they her. The streets were bustling with activity, and it was easy to become lost in the hustle and bustle of the afternoon. She was almost blinded by the glistening reflection from the harbor when she took a moment to look up, marveling at its vast expanse. Suddenly, Ariel noticed two men in suits standing next to Miles, who was crouched on a docked sailboat. Ariel started to walk toward him but then hesitated, not wanting to intrude on what seemed like an intense conversation.

He looked upset, and Ariel wondered if these men had anything to do with his ex-wife. Before she could turn and walk away, Miles looked up from his conversation, and their eyes met. Ariel felt her cheeks flame with embarrassment. Miles nodded to her and raised a hand. He spoke briefly to the men again, and they drifted away from him.

She walked up to Miles once the men were gone, completely forgetting that she had been on her way to get lunch.

"Miles?" she said softly, feeling a pang of sadness in her chest at his expression of despair. "Are you okay?"

Miles looked away for a moment before finally meeting her gaze with a sigh. "No, actually. Those were my ex-wife's lawyers. They're here to serve me papers regarding our divorce settlement. Apparently, she wants more than what we discussed months ago." He jumped down from the boat to the dock, coming to stand beside her.

He paused for a moment, before continuing in a bitter voice. "The truth is I can't afford it, and now I'm going to be stuck paying for something I don't want or even need. It's going to delay my plans for the slip." He gazed off into the distance, looking distraught.

Ariel felt terrible for him. She knew how hard it must have been for him not only emotionally but financially too. She put her hand on his shoulder in an attempt to comfort him, squeezing it gently.

He turned toward Ariel with an apologetic smile on his face. "I'm sorry you had to see that. It isn't exactly something I want aired out in public," he said softly as he ran a hand through his hair in frustration.

"Trust me, I know all about having your problems aired. I just came from the mayor's office."

Miles's eyes widened, "Wait, what did you need to talk to the mayor about?"

Ariel sighed and looked away for a moment before finally speaking. "It was about Katie. I found out she's been getting bullied at school, and I wanted to see if the mayor could help in any way. It's his hooligan son who's doing the bullying."

Miles nodded slowly, understanding finally settling in his expression. "He was with those kids the other night? That makes sense," he said quietly. "I've seen him—his name is Connor—around the harbor with his rowdy friends. They're your typical privileged, rich kids. Can I help at all?"

The two of them stood there silently for a few moments. Ariel's hand was still resting on his shoulder as they both gazed out at the twinkling harbor. She felt her heart swell with admiration for him. Even through such difficult times, he was here trying to help other people too.

"No, there's nothing you can do," she said finally, her voice strong with conviction. "But I would like to thank you for trying and offer you lunch as a gesture of appreciation. I could really use a friend."

Miles chuckled softly and shook his head. "Thanks for the offer— and how interesting that you think of us as friends. My charm must be working already."

"Oh? Were you applying it?"

"As hard as I could," he admitted, his white teeth flashing. "Unfortunately, I still have a ton of work to do before I come over and help with the porch reconstruction. But don't worry, I'll be there soon enough. Now, go get that lunch, it's been a long day."

Ariel smiled widely. Knowing he was still planning on coming over despite his own problems was enough to make her feel better about things.

"That sounds perfect," she said happily as she gave him one last pat on the shoulder before she started walking toward the harbor cafe.

***

The Throwback Diner was a blast from the past, with its bright neon sign, chrome accents, and vintage decor. The black-and-white checkered floor gleamed under the flicker of the neon lights, and the counter was a long stretch of polished chrome and red vinyl. The smell of freshly brewed coffee and grilling burgers filled the air, as the patrons chatted and laughed over plates of classic diner food. The waitstaff, dressed in traditional diner uniforms, bustled around taking orders and refilling drinks. The jukebox in the corner played hits from the fifties and sixties, adding to the nostalgic atmosphere. Overall, the diner was a cozy, welcoming spot that transported its customers back in time.

Ariel walked into the diner, her head down and her thoughts heavy with worry. She made her way to an empty booth in the corner, sliding into the worn leather seat. As she sat down, the weight of her recent struggles settled noticeably on her shoulders.

The waitress from Ariel's first visit, Jill, approached her table with a warm smile. "Hey hon, what can I get for you today?"

Ariel let out a sigh. "Just a coffee for now, thanks. And call me Ariel."

Jill's smile faltered as she noticed the sadness etched on Ariel's face. "Is everything okay? You look upset."

Ariel let out a small laugh. "Just a rough day, that's all. But I'll be fine."

Jill nodded understandingly. "Well, let me know if you need anything else. I'll bring that coffee right out for you. Remember, we serve breakfast all day."

As Jill walked away, Ariel felt a twinge of gratitude for the kind waitress. She leaned her head against her hand and let out a deep breath, trying to push away her worries and focus on the present moment.

Jill returned shortly with the coffee, and Ariel ordered a crab omelet. Before she walked away to put in the order, Jill hesitated. "Maybe this isn't my business, but you should be careful around Miles Clemens—I saw you two talking."

As Ariel took a sip of her coffee, Jill's words echoed, making Ariel feel uneasy. She'd been a bit wary of Miles, but she couldn't deny that he'd been a big help with the house, and she was grateful for it.

"What do you mean, be careful of Miles?" Ariel asked.

Jill leaned in conspiratorially. "I heard he's got a dark past. Some say he did time for murder. But I don't know if that's true or just small-town gossip."

Ariel's eyes widened in shock. "Murder? That's a pretty serious accusation." And it was almost amusing how the gossip grew—first, he was a secret billionaire who'd philandered on his poor, unsuspecting spouse. Now, the woman was in her grave, and he was just tending sailboats in Maine. Interesting.

Jill shrugged. "Like I said, I don't know if it's true or not. But I just thought you should know in case it is. You're new here, and you've got a lot on your plate already with that old house of yours."

"I mean, I don't know what's worse. Flirting with a possible murderer or getting hit on by the mayor."

Jill pulled a face. "Ew. Well, at least Mayor Stanton is an open book. He wants more money, more power, and wife number four. But Miles—man, he's a good-looking devil, but no one around here knows what to make of him."

With that, Jill trotted off to put in Ariel's order. Ariel, her head reeling from her crazy day, picked up the dessert menu nearby and thought that the day called for dessert after lunch—and maybe two desserts.

CHAPTER TWENTY TWO

That evening at home, Katie sat on the bathroom counter in one of the downstairs bathrooms, feet swinging as she chattered happily to Ariel. As Ariel scraped wallpaper, Katie gushed, "And Connor even came up to me and apologized. Can you believe it? He invited me out with his friends tonight, but I actually have a ton of homework. He asked twice if I would go!"

What did his dad say to him? Ariel wondered.

The sun was setting, casting warm light through the windows of their cozy home as they worked together. Ariel stopped for a moment to admire how peaceful it felt in that moment—just her and her daughter, and the sound of the scraper and Katie's feet swinging as Ariel worked on this familiar task.

Ariel hummed softly as she peeled away a long section of old wallpaper from the wall. "And I found out that there is a debate club here, and that I can swap out shop class for Drama *if* you say it's okay."

"Of course. That sounds like a good trade to me."

As they talked, Ariel noticed how Katie's eyes seemed a bit brighter and more cheerful than usual, and it made her heart swell with joy.

Katie rushed on, "And Mom, did you know that Cara from my class moved here from out of state? She said she used to live in a huge mansion! Can you believe it? She's really cool."

Ariel paused and looked up at her daughter, who was busy marveling at all these new experiences. "That sounds like an exciting place, doesn't it?" she asked gently.

Katie nodded eagerly, eyes wide with wonderment. "She said there were secret passages hidden behind the walls! Can you imagine that? Maybe we could find something like that here, too, if we look hard enough!"

Ariel smiled indulgently and ruffled Katie's hair fondly as she continued working on scraping away bits of wallpaper from around the edges of window frames and doorways. As they worked side by side, Ariel thought about all the possibilities hidden behind those walls— tales of adventure and mystery. Maybe Katie could make memories here like Ariel and Charlie had as kids.

The light was fading outside as they discussed paint colors for the dining room and whether or not they should put up drapes in the living room when suddenly there was a loud bang coming from downstairs—a thump which echoed through every corner of the house. Both mother and daughter shared a nervous glance before quickly jumping up and racing downstairs to investigate.

When they arrived downstairs, both were relieved that nothing looked out of place or disturbed—save for one thing: their window near their back door had been broken open from an outside source, but nothing seemed amiss on either side of the windowpane itself. It almost seemed as though someone had tried to get into their home, but why? Ariel set about finding out what was going on.

Ariel and Katie quickly scanned the room, looking for any signs of intrusion or damage. Ariel's heart was racing, and she could see that Katie was visibly shaken by the loud noise. "It's okay, sweetie," Ariel said, trying to keep her voice calm. "Let's just check the rest of the house and make sure everything is okay."

They walked through the rooms, checking windows and doors, but everything seemed to be in order. Ariel couldn't let go of the feeling of unease as she thought about the broken window and the possible implications of someone trying to break into their home.

"Let's go check the back door," Ariel said, leading the way to the kitchen. As they approached the back door, Ariel could see that the window next to it was shattered, shards of glass scattered across the floor. She quickly scanned the area outside, but there was no sign of anyone or anything suspicious.

"Oh my god," Katie breathed, her eyes wide with fear. "What if someone was trying to break in?"

Ariel put an arm around her daughter, trying to comfort her. "It's okay, we're safe. I'll call the police and report it, but I'm sure it was just a random act of vandalism. We'll get the window fixed and make sure everything is secure."

As Ariel made the call to the police, suspicion swirled in her mind—something more was going on. Someone was trying to intimidate her and her family, and she knew that she would have to be extra vigilant from now on.

She thought about calling Charlie, but Ariel knew her sister would raise cane until Ariel came to stay at her house. And though Ariel would be grateful for the offer, she felt like doing so would be giving the vandals what they wanted—sending her and Katie running.

Suddenly, Ariel remembered that she had Miles's business card. She dug through her wallet until she found it and dialed his number. As it rang, she hoped that he would answer, and she could tell him what happened and ask if he could come help board up the windows.

When Miles answered the phone, Ariel quickly briefed him on the situation. "Someone broke into our house, and I'm scared. Please come help me board up the windows."

Miles answered with a firm, reassuring voice, "Don't worry, I'm coming right over."

Ariel hung up the phone in relief and quickly gathered some plywood from their garage and waited for Miles to arrive. Twenty minutes later, Miles pulled up in his truck, just as the police were leaving after taking their report about the vandalism.

"Thanks for coming," Ariel said, grateful for his quick response. She showed him where the broken window was located, and Miles carefully surveyed the area, peering into the darkness through his flashlight as he made sure that there were no suspicious characters lurking around.

"Did the police check the house?" he asked. When Ariel nodded, he let out a breath.

"Looks like you two are safe," Miles declared after a few more minutes of scanning. He set about boarding up the broken window with nails and screws while Ariel worked on covering up the other one.

It didn't take long until both windows were securely boarded up against any further intruders or vandals. Katie seemed somewhat calmer now that they had taken action to protect themselves against any potential danger.

"I'm worried something else could happen during the night," Miles said, pulling Ariel into the kitchen where Katie couldn't overhear.

"You don't have to stay," Ariel replied. "You must be exhausted from your shift at work today."

"I want to stay," Miles reassured. "I'll sleep on the couch—or in my truck, even."

Ariel hesitated before replying. "If you're sure it won't be too much trouble …"

Miles smiled and nodded. "It's no trouble at all."

"But not in your truck. Goodness! The couch is comfy, and the heat works now, so you should be okay there."

Reassured when they told her that Miles was staying, Katie trudged up to bed, homework forgotten in her exhaustion. Ariel would get up early to help her. She needed rest after the night they'd had.

An inviting fire cast a warm glow over the living room, illuminating the two figures sitting on the couch before it. The fire snapped and crackled in the hearth as Miles and Ariel sipped their drinks in silence. She began to tell him the story of all the strange happenings at Leeside, from Doris to the lurker to now, with the bricks. He listened, frowning softly.

"What do you think?" she asked.

"I think Charlene is right about Doris—she's harmless, though there might be something there you could ask about in regard to your father. But the lurker and the bricks? I have a sneaking suspicion that Stanton is trying to intimidate you."

"That's what I'm afraid of," Ariel admitted. "And will the police do anything?"

Miles shrugged. "For now, it's some broken glass and shaken nerves. They have no one to pin it on, and no one got hurt. I'm not saying it's right, but they're not exactly going to work on your case around the clock."

Ariel sighed. "Yup. Another thing I was afraid of."

They lapsed into silence. Ariel broke the silence, her voice soft and curious, "Tell me about what brought you to Endless Harbor," she asked, her eyes never leaving his.

Miles sighed and cleared his throat, his gaze flitting away from her own. "It's complicated," he said, his voice heavy with emotion. "And to be honest, quite painful."

She gathered her courage. It was time to tell him her story. "Miles, I know we've only known each other for a short while, but I feel like I can trust you. I want to tell you why I left Miami and why I'm in Endless Harbor."

Miles looked at her with a concerned expression. "Of course, Ariel. I'm here to listen."

Ariel hesitated for a moment before continuing, "I was fired from my bigwig corporate job. I was one of the top executives, but I was let go because the owner's slimeball son didn't like that I challenged a new company initiative. It was a huge blow to my ego and my confidence. And then, to make matters worse, my ex-boyfriend cheated on me and dumped me. For a woman named Mitzi. I was just at rock bottom, and I needed to get away from it all."

Miles listened intently, nodding along as she spoke. When she finished, he placed a comforting hand on her shoulder and said, "I'm sorry you had to go through all of that. But you should know that you're not alone, Ariel. I know what it's like to hit rock bottom and feel like you have nowhere to turn. But you're here now, and you're making something of yourself. You're strong, and you're going to make it."

Ariel felt a weight lifted off her shoulders as she heard Miles's words of encouragement. She smiled at him. "Thank you, Miles. I really appreciate it. I left all that drama behind in Miami, but now I just wish I could find some kind of peace," Ariel said, sighing.

Miles put his hand over hers. "It's out there," he said softly. "You just have to keep searching for it. And you know what? I think you might find it here, despite all of this. You were made to be here, in this house by the sea. *Ariel*, even."

She laughed. It wasn't the first time her childhood on the coast had drawn cartoon mermaid comparisons. Her father had even called her his undersea princess.

The conversation lulled as they both sipped their glasses of wine slowly, watching the hearth crackle. His hand remined over hers. The atmosphere between them seemed charged now; Ariel could feel an undercurrent of tension that hadn't been there earlier.

Suddenly, without warning, Miles leaned over and brushed his lips softly against her cheek before quickly pulling away with a sheepish smile on his face. Ariel felt her cheeks heating up. She hadn't expected it, but she couldn't deny that she was strangely drawn to this man who had saved her from danger earlier that evening.

Suddenly, Ariel noticed an orange glow from outside the window—it wasn't the fire in the fireplace! She gasped and leaped from her seat just in time to see flames engulfing the side of the house.

CHAPTER TWENTY THREE

Ariel almost cried out when they came around the side of the house, both running. The dry bushes planted there were aflame—but, luckily, the fire hadn't gotten to the house itself.

"There!" Miles pointed to the ground just past the bushes. Ariel was off and running. Miraculously, the rusty spigot on that side of the house was actually working, and it wasn't frozen over. Miles grabbed the ancient hose that was attached to it and ran out, uncoiling the cracked rubber tubing. Ariel wrenched the tap all the way open, and with a whine, and after what seemed like an eternity, water burst from the metal end. He aimed the water at the base of the hedge, where the flames seemed to be the most intense.

Ariel grabbed a nearby bucket and began gathering water from a significant leak in the hose, throwing it on the flames as well. Together, they worked to put out the fire, their determination to save the hedge and the house giving them strength.

The fire was hot, and the smoke was thick, making it hard to see. But Miles and Ariel didn't give up. They worked tirelessly, dousing the hedge with water until, finally, the flames were out. The hedge was a bit charred and smoky, but it was still standing.

Miles and Ariel stood outside of the house, staring at the smoldering remains of the bushes that had been set on fire. The fire was gone, but Ariel had a newfound sense of unease—just when she was settling from the broken windows.

"I'm pretty sure this was arson," Miles said, pointing to a few singed branches that were still smoldering. "See how the fire spread in a pattern? And it looks like it started in multiple places, not one. It wasn't natural; it was deliberately set."

Ariel's heart sank as she took in the damage. "Are you sure?"

"I've seen my fair share of fires," Miles said, his expression serious. "Not something that's pretty when you're in a floating vessel in the middle of an ocean. So, you get really good at preventing them and spotting what went wrong when they happen. And this one was definitely set on purpose. Whoever did this knew what they were doing."

"I won't let someone drive me out of my own home. Not even that slimy mayor."

Ariel couldn't believe that the mayor and his cronies would stoop to such a level. Her heart raced at the thought of what could have happened to Katie. What if Connor, the mayor's son, had something to do with the fire? Maybe asking Katie out tonight was a way to get her out of the house. So, did that make him part of it or someone trying to prevent Katie from getting hurt by it?

"I'd understand if you want to call it quits," Miles said. "This is way beyond a little red tape."

But Ariel had come too far to back down now. "I'm going to call the police back and report this," she said, her voice shaking with anger and determination. "I won't let him get away with this."

Miles nodded, his expression serious. "I'll help you however I can."

Together, they made the call to the police and waited for them to arrive. As they waited, Ariel tried to tamp down her anxiety. The mayor was willing to go to great lengths to stop her from opening her B&B, what else would he be capable of? But with Miles supporting her, she felt a little bit more confident that they could take him on.

As they walked away from the ashes of the bushes, toward the police cruiser that was inching up the driveway, Ariel couldn't shake off the feeling of betrayal. But she knew she couldn't dwell on it now. There was too much at stake, and she had to stay focused if she wanted to come out on top. If she didn't buckle under the pressure—if she just stayed the course—Ariel knew she had a fighting chance.

CHAPTER TWENTY FOUR

The mayor just might get away with it.

Ariel pushed down her anger and tried to stay busy with renovations while preparing her second presentation for the board to get permission to open her B&B. As she walked through town a few days later, she could feel the life coming back into the harbor. Boats were slipping out of their berths one by one, and Ariel let a pang of sadness linger, a bittersweet feeling taking hold of her at how quickly time was moving. She had worked day and night to make sure Leeside would be ready for its grand opening later in the summer.

There had been no developments on the fire at the house—though the police had agreed that it looked intentionally set, there hadn't been enough evidence left behind to catch the culprit. In fact, any evidence that there might have been—footprints, for example—had been tainted by the gallons and gallons of water that Ariel and Miles had sent gushing from the hose to extinguish the blaze that night. But nothing else had happened in the time since, and Ariel now faithfully monitored the camera system she had set up around the property.

So, she hadn't caught anyone and had no evidence that Stanton had been involved. Did that mean he would look squeaky clean at the next presentation?

As she passed the drugstore next to the Throwback Diner, Ariel was surprised by a Valentine's Day display. Time was flying by in a blur of hammering, sawing, and painting as Ariel handily transformed the building from a ramshackle house into a charming bed and breakfast, so the holiday had snuck up on her. She'd also worked on data-filled, well-researched presentation materials to present to the board to gain permission to open up the business—all while trying not to think of Dylan, who'd dumped her on the last major celebration day in her life.

But this Valentine's Day wouldn't be like her birthday—Miles was here, too, his warm presence a reminder that good things could often come out of bad experiences. The two had worked together boarding up the windows that a vandal had broken while trying to get into their house during an especially dark night and then he'd stayed over so

Ariel and Katie could feel safe. She thought about it a lot since, about what a sweet gesture that had been.

Later that day, Ariel stood in the gleaming kitchen of Leeside, and she was still thinking of those acts of kindness. Though she was alone, she smiled in gratitude as she recalled Miles's determination to protect them from harm; his kindness helping her through such a vulnerable moment when everything seemed bleak and uncertain. Now that they had made it through the winter months, Ariel felt hopeful about what was ahead as they moved forward with planning the operations of the inn, which would soon be ready to welcome guests at long last.

Miles stopped by often after his shifts were over at the marina, or when he had some free time on weekends. He helped with refinishing floors, moving furniture around, or anything heavy that needed lifting. His presence was always welcome, and it provided much-needed assistance for everything that still needed doing before her grand opening could take place.

Kurt, Charlene, and the kids were regular fixtures as well, and not only did being surrounded by family begin to help Katie, but Kurt and Miles had formed a friendship, and they tackled bigger home projects at Leeside together. Charlene had even stopped reporting on the latest scandal involving Miles, though Ariel did occasionally miss whatever the gossip of the week was. She had last heard that Miles was an ex-mobster who was living in Endless Harbor under an assumed name because three known gangs from the West Coast had put out hits on him.

When Charlene had carried that tale, Ariel had been watching the so-called gangster play fetch with Rufus. She had trouble believing that the same man who was out there jiggling the jowls of a drooly Great Dane and baby-talking him could be a stone-cold mobster.

The days flew by quickly; she couldn't believe how much progress she had made so far. Soon enough, she would finally have her own business which she could proudly call her own—a dream come true. Her menu was coming together, thanks to the upgraded kitchen that the funds from the Miami house had afforded her.

They had managed to get so much done that Ariel had been doubtful about because of the complete lack of extra tradesman around. But the guys had done the heavy lifting, Kurt's expertise had allowed them to avoid mistakes, and the result was the chef's kitchen of Ariel's dreams. As April came around, there would be only a few more weeks until all renovations would be complete—and then they could start decorating!

The new, gourmet, modern kitchen in the renovated Victorian house was a sight to behold. The space had been completely gutted and rebuilt to include all the latest amenities. The cabinets were a sleek, glossy white, with stainless-steel handles. The countertops were made of a polished granite that shone in the light, and the backsplash was made of shimmering, iridescent glass tiles. The appliances were all high-end, including a six-burner gas range with a griddle, a double oven, and a built-in refrigerator with a bottom freezer. A large island in the center of the room provided ample workspace, and a built-in wine cooler and bar sink would make entertaining a breeze. The floors were made of wide-plank, reclaimed hardwood that had been stained a warm, rich color. Large windows let in natural light and provided a picturesque view of the garden outside. The whole space had a feeling of warmth and elegance, making it the perfect place to cook, entertain, and enjoy.

Ariel felt a rush of excitement as she moved around the kitchen. The gleaming stainless-steel appliances and granite countertops were a stark contrast to the fast-paced, corporate kitchens she had grown accustomed to. As she began to gather ingredients and prep her dishes, she found herself lost in the familiar rhythms of cooking. The chop of a knife against a cutting board, the sizzle of butter in a pan, and the aroma of herbs and spices filled the air. She had almost forgotten how much she loved the art of cooking and the satisfaction of creating a delicious meal. The kitchen felt like a sanctuary, a place where she could let her creativity flow and escape the stresses of the outside world. She realized that she had been missing this feeling for far too long, and she vowed to make sure she would never lose it again.

Ariel's phone rang, and she hesitated before answering it. She recognized the number, and it made her throat close in panic, but she answered it anyway. "Hello?"

"Ariel, it's Dylan," the voice on the other end said.

Ariel's heart sank. She hadn't heard from her ex-boyfriend in months, and she had hoped that she would never hear from him again. "What do you want?" she asked, trying to keep her voice steady.

"I made a mistake," Dylan said. "Mitzi left me for a younger guy, and I realize now that I never should have let you go."

Ariel rolled her eyes. "You think I'm just going to take you back because Mitzi left you?" she asked, her anger rising. "You broke my heart, Dylan. And now you expect me to just forgive and forget? Why don't you go ask the partners at your firm to keep you warm at night?"

"I know I messed up," Dylan said, sounding desperate. "But I love you, Ariel. Please, give me another chance."

"No," Ariel said firmly. "I deserve better than someone who would treat me like you did. And besides, I've moved on. I have a life here, and I'm not going to let you come in and mess it up."

"Ariel, please," Dylan begged. "I know you. You can't be happy in that nothing town. What could be there for you that's not in Miami?"

Ariel looked around her kitchen. There were so many things here that were not in Miami—the cool Eastern seas, her sister, Kurt, and the kids. Endless Harbor, despite its foibles. And Miles.

"I'm sorry, Dylan," Ariel said, her tone softening. "But my father's house is here. And I'm staying for it. My answer is no. Good luck with everything."

And with that, Ariel hung up the phone and took a deep breath, feeling a sense of closure and empowerment wash over her. She was done with Dylan, and she could finally move on with her life. She stood at the kitchen island in shock. Her trance was interrupted when Miles knocked on the door. Ariel fussed around for a moment, making sure she'd turned off all the burners, and opened the front door, her hair pulled back in a messy bun and pink smudged on her cheeks from the heat of the kitchen.

"Hey Miles, what's up?" she asked, thrilled to see him.

"Reporting for floor duty," Miles said and then sniffed the air. "Are you cooking?"

"I am, but it's not ready for prime time yet. But I think I was just about to need a break," Ariel said, rubbing her temples.

"You okay?"

She blew out a breath. "Not really." She waved her phone, which she tucked into her jeans pocket before she took off her kitchen apron and tossed it on an entryway table. "Honestly, my ex just called me. And it sucked. You know how that goes?"

"I'm sorry, Ariel," Miles said, reaching out to touch her arm in a comforting gesture. "I know it's tough, but you don't have to go through this alone. And, oh boy, do I know how that goes."

Ariel forced a smile. "Thanks, Miles. I appreciate it. But I think I just need to take a step back and regroup. Maybe go for a walk by the harbor and clear my head."

"That's a good idea," Miles said, nodding. "I was hoping you would say that. Let's go."

"What?"

"I have something to show you," he said, a mysterious smile on his face. "Something I've been cooking up myself."

Ariel hesitated for a moment, but the idea of getting out of the house and going for a walk with Miles was too tempting. "Okay, let me just grab my coat," she said and followed Miles out the door.

As they walked, Miles pointed out the signs of spring starting to peek through the cold winter weather. The ice on the harbor was slowly melting, and the first boats of the season were starting to come out of their berths along the strip of shore near Leeside. Ariel felt her hope renewed as she took in the sights and sounds of the sea.

Miles then led her to the small cove that belonged to her property, hidden behind large rocks and sheltered by tall pines. There Ariel found three small, wooden boats, all freshly painted and varnished, waiting to be launched. They were tied to sturdy posts sunk into the beach, and they bobbed like jewels in the water.

"It's not the full-on slip I envisioned," he said, "but I built them for you. For your B&B, so your guests can take them out for a spin."

Ariel couldn't believe it; she was touched and speechless. She hugged Miles tightly, unable to find the words to thank him for his kind gesture.

"There's one more thing," he said, drawing away from her embrace. He pointed, and Ariel could see that Miles had set up an elaborate picnic lunch on a large blanket, complete with a white tablecloth, candlesticks, and a bouquet of flowers. The spread included a variety of sandwiches, cheeses, fruits, and a bottle of wine chilling in a bucket of ice.

A basket of fresh croissants was placed next to a bowl of mixed berries and whipped cream. The sun was shining, and the breeze was blowing through the sailboats, making it the perfect setting for a romantic lunch. Miles had also set up a portable Bluetooth speaker, playing soft music that added to the ambiance of the moment.

Ariel smiled at the effort Miles had put into this surprise picnic. She was touched by his thoughtfulness and care. "Miles, this is amazing," Ariel said, admiring the spread before her. "Thank you so much for doing this."

"I wanted to do something special for you," Miles said, taking her hand and leading her to sit down. "You've been working so hard. I just wanted to make it a little bit better."

As they sat and enjoyed their lunch, Ariel told him all about growing up in Endless Harbor and how much she loved the town and its history. Ariel felt grateful for Miles's company and the distraction from her thoughts. She felt her spirits lifted, and her worries melted away. Together, they watched the boats come and go, enjoying the warm sun and the swish of the water lapping against the shore. It was a perfect day, and Ariel felt grateful for the special memories she was making with Miles.

As they sat by the boats, Miles poured Ariel a glass of wine and handed her a plate of delicious food. "I have something more to tell you," he said, looking out at the water. "I know you've been curious about my past, and I want to be honest with you."

Ariel put down her fork and listened attentively.

"I used to have a speed boat manufacturing business," he began. "It was successful, and I was making a good living. But then the economy crashed. I thought the business had enough to float through the rough patch, but then I found out that my business partner had decided to spend the company's money in some very unsavory ways. He spent time in prison for embezzlement and fraud, but I lost everything. My wife left me, and I was left with nothing. I've been trying to rebuild my life ever since."

Ariel's heart went out to Miles. She couldn't imagine going through something like that. "I'm so sorry, Miles," she said, reaching out to touch his hand. "I had no idea. But I'm glad you're here now."

Miles looked at Ariel and smiled, "Me too. I came back to what I love—being on the water, working with boats, and building again. And I'm glad I can be here for you and help you with your B&B. I know how important this is to you, and I want to be a part of making it happen."

Ariel smiled back at him.

"Now, how many of the really dirty details of my professional and personal implosion do you want?" Miles asked, biting into a strawberry.

Ariel laughed. "All of them, of course."

She grabbed for a croissant, feeling grateful for his support and understanding—and now, his vulnerability. She realized that she had found a true friend in Miles, someone who truly cared about her and her dreams.

But could they be more than friends? And was that something that Ariel was even considering?

Her chest fluttered.

She wouldn't rule it out just yet.

CHAPTER TWENTY FIVE

"Three dozen?"

"Three dozen boats," he said. "And the demand for them was so high that they commanded a hefty, celebrity-level price. Everything was done by hand. They were true works of art."

"And you couldn't start that back up again—building the bigger boats?"

He shrugged and tossed a bit of croissant out to a swooping seagull. "It would take a lot of collateral to start back up. And I have the divorce still dragging on and ..." he hesitated. "Honestly, Ari, I still owe a lot of people from when my old company went under."

"But you said it's been years!"

"I'm still paying them back. It's slow, and not ideal, but I'm going to make sure all of my debts are paid."

The Maine shore during a spring day was a picturesque sight to behold. As their picnic wound down, the sun was shining down on the water, casting a bright and warm glow on the surface. The ocean was a deep blue, and the waves were gently lapping against the shore. The sand was a soft, warm white, and the salty sea air was invigorating. The sky was a brilliant shade of blue with fluffy, white clouds lazily drifting by. Seagulls were calling out to one another as they soared overhead, and the rhythm of the waves was a soothing background noise. Ariel took in all of the natural beauty around her, feeling a sense of peace wash over her as she watched the shore. The harsh winter was now a distant memory, and the promise of a new season was invigorating.

Ariel looked slyly over at Miles. "You know, rumors in town are that you are a notorious playboy who jilted your wife for probably three dozen lovers."

"Only three dozen?" He laughed, his eyes flashing and the corners of his eyes crinkling.

"Depends on who you ask. Some people think you killed her and are hiding out here."

His eyes widened. "No way. My ex is very much happy and remarried and living in Cape Cod. But I sound a lot more like a movie bad boy if you believe the rumors. Maybe that's not a bad thing."

"I like nice guys," Ariel said, smiling shyly.

Ariel stole glances at Miles as they sat on the shore. He was always so put together, and even now, with his hair blowing in the breeze and a bit of salt spray on his face, he looked handsome. There was a distinct flutter in her stomach as she thought about how thoughtful he was.

Miles met her gaze, and she could see the romantic intent in his eyes. He looked at her with a mixture of tenderness and longing, and she let herself linger on the spark of attraction she felt for him. She felt a connection with him that she had not felt with anyone else in a long time. As she looked into his eyes, she knew that he felt the same way about her.

Again, the palpable tension between them grew and neither wanted to break it. She couldn't deny the chemistry between them, but she couldn't stop the memory of her past relationships and the hurt they had caused her from creeping in. She knew Miles had also been hurt in the past, and she wondered if they were both just setting themselves up for more heartache. But as she looked at him, a wave of gratitude for the time they were spending together now suffused her. She decided to push her worries aside and just enjoy the moment.

Looking at her watch, she realized she had to be back for Katie getting home from school, and she still had to put the finishing touches on the board presentation. She was feeling more and more nervous with each passing minute. She ran her fingers through her hair as her voice wavered when she spoke. "I'm really nervous about the presentation," she said.

Miles smiled reassuringly and gave a playful wink. "Don't worry about it, leave it to me."

"Why? Are the board members afraid of you because of your mad killer reputation?"

"No. All the ladies on the board are among my three dozen lovers. So, you could say I have influence."

Ariel laughed, and as they packed up the picnic, she realized that she was content—something she hadn't been in a long time. Or maybe something that she hadn't *stopped* to realize. She looked over at Miles, who was carefully folding the blanket, and she noticed the way the sun danced in his hair, making him look even more handsome than usual. She couldn't believe he'd built her those boats as a Valentine's Day gift. They were the most thoughtful present she had ever received, and she couldn't wait to take them out on the water.

As they left the beach and made their way back to Leeside, Ariel thought hard about how she might shake off the fear of getting hurt

114

again. But as she reached out and grabbed Miles's hand, she realized that she didn't have to think about the future right now. They could just enjoy the time they had together. And so, they walked hand in hand back to his truck, their steps in sync, content in each other's company.

CHAPTER TWENTY SIX

"Mom, the weirdest thing happened today," Katie said as she sat at the kitchen table that night while Ariel prepared dinner. "Connor, the mayor's son, asked me out on a date."

Ariel's heart sank. She had suspected that the mayor and his sycophants were behind the arson attempt on her B&B, and now she couldn't shake the feeling that Connor had something to do with it. "Really? What did you say to him?"

"I told him I would think about it," Katie replied, looking up at her mom with a mix of excitement and uncertainty.

"I don't know, Katie," Ariel said, her mind racing with thoughts of potential danger. "We don't know what the mayor and his family are capable of."

"I know, Mom," Katie said, looking down at her hands. "The brick. The fire. But I don't think Connor would do that. I really like him. And he seemed genuinely sorry for the way his friends treated me at school. Actually, he totally ditched his friends, and he hasn't been hanging with the kid who was mean to me about being from Miami."

Ariel blinked, shaking her head as though she hadn't heard Katie quite right. "Wait, Connor wasn't the one who said that?"

"No. He just stood there. But he didn't stick up for me or tell them to stop, so he definitely had something to say sorry for."

Ariel felt the barest glimmer of hope—maybe Connor wasn't the hooligan she'd judged him to be. She could be wrong, just as Endless Harbor had been wrong about Miles.

"Just be careful, okay? I don't want you to get hurt."

"I will, Mom," Katie said, giving her a reassuring smile. "I promise."

As Katie chattered on about her day at school, Ariel's mind was elsewhere. She was awash with the uplifting feeling of being no longer the same woman she'd left behind in Miami. She had grown and evolved, and she was proud of herself and of Katie.

She looked over at Katie, who was looking at her curiously.

"Mom, is something wrong?" Katie asked, noticing her mother's distraction.

Ariel smiled and reached over to tousle her daughter's hair. "Don't worry, sweetie," she said. Then, remembering, she added, "I have a big meeting tomorrow with the board to get final permission to open up the bed and breakfast."

Katie's face softened. "I hope it goes well. You deserve good things, Mom."

Ariel's eyes widened in surprise. It was the first sign of appreciation that Katie had shown for her in a long time—since their tension about the newest bullying situation.

"Thank you, Katie," Ariel said, reaching across the table to take her daughter's hand. "I really appreciate that."

"I know things have been tough for us, but I'm really proud of you for going for this. You're not just doing it for yourself, you're doing it for us too," Katie said, a hint of a smile on her face. "And I'm not always saying it, but I see it."

Ariel felt her heart swell with emotion. "I love you, Katie," she said, tears welling up in her eyes.

"I love you, too, Mom," Katie replied, and they shared a warm smile across the table.

The heart-to-heart left Ariel feeling happy, and she felt more confident going into her big meeting the next day. She knew that she had her daughter's support, and that meant everything to her.

After dinner, Ariel decided to do something special. She had been so focused on the renovations and the presentation that she had let her love for cooking fall by the wayside. So, she pulled out her old, Parisian pasty knowledge and began to bake something fancy. It had been a long time since she had baked anything other than serviceable meals, but as she mixed and measured, she warmed with her rediscovered love for the culinary arts.

Ariel rummaged through her cabinets, pulling out all of the ingredients she would need for her recipe. She had been craving a French apple tart for days now, and she finally had the time to make one. She carefully measured out the flour, sugar, and butter, mixing them together in a large bowl until they formed a crumbly dough. She pressed the dough into a tart pan, making sure to evenly distribute it across the bottom and up the sides.

Next, she prepared the filling. She peeled and thinly sliced Granny Smith apples, then tossed them in a mixture of sugar, cinnamon, and a splash of lemon juice. She arranged the slices in a beautiful pattern on top of the crust, careful to keep the edges slightly overlapping. She then sprinkled some more sugar and cinnamon on top and placed the tart in the oven.

As the tart baked, the aroma of apples and cinnamon filled the kitchen. Ariel inhaled deeply and smiled, feeling a sense of satisfaction wash over her. She had always loved baking, and it had been a long time since she had taken the time to make something fancy. She realized that with her new B&B business, she could incorporate her love of cooking into the experience for her guests.

She thought about designing gourmet menus featuring the local seafood and produce, with a French twist. She could offer cooking classes for her guests or even host dinner parties. The possibilities were endless, and it made her even more excited about her new venture.

Once the tart was done, she carefully removed it from the oven and let it cool on a wire rack. She couldn't wait to take a bite, the golden-brown crust was perfectly flaky, and the filling was bubbling and fragrant. She knew this would be a hit with her guests; she was probably going to include it in her future menu.

As Ariel carefully removed the French apple tart from the oven, the aroma of buttery crust and caramelized apples filled the kitchen. Katie, who had been sitting at the kitchen table doing her homework, looked up and sniffed the air. "Wow, Mom, that smells amazing," she said, her eyes lighting up.

Ariel grinned as she set the tart on the counter to cool. "I thought I'd try something a little fancy tonight. I've been thinking about designing gourmet menus for the guests at the B&B, and I wanted to test out some recipes."

Katie got up from her chair and walked over to the counter, peering at the tart with interest. "I've never really known you to be such a great cook," she said, surprised. "I mean, I know you were in France, and I know you went to culinary school, but you never really—well, we ate a lot of takeout in Miami."

Ariel laughed. "I've had a lot of time on my hands since we moved here. And I've always loved cooking, it's just that I didn't have much time for it before. But with the B&B, I want to make sure that the guests have an unforgettable experience. And that includes the food. You can be my taste tester for everything."

"Well, I can't wait to try it," Katie said, her face eager.

Ariel smiled, cut her a slice, and watched as Katie took a bite. Her eyes widened in pleasure, and she let out a moan of satisfaction. "Mom, this is incredible. You have to make this for the guests at the B&B."

Ariel felt a warmth spread through her chest, happy that Katie was finally showing an interest and appreciation for all the hard work she had been putting in. "I'll definitely consider it," she said with a smile.

As she sat down to enjoy her tart, Ariel reveled in the excitement of what the future held for her and her B&B. She had her daughter's support, a new business to look forward to, and her passion for cooking to keep her company. Everything was finally falling into place.

CHAPTER TWENTY SEVEN

The night for the final meeting had arrived. Ariel walked into town hall. Despite having been through this once, her heart was pounding with nerves. She had spent the last few days preparing for this meeting, making sure all her documents were in order, and her argument was solid. And there had been few people at the last meeting. But as she looked around the room, she saw that it was now packed with people.

Mayor Stanton was there, as expected, surrounded by men in suits from the giant corporations, all there to argue their case. But what surprised Ariel the most was the number of people from the town who had also shown up to support her and her B&B.

She saw familiar faces from the diner, the hardware store, and even the school where Katie went. They were all there, holding signs and cheering her on. Was this the rebel crew that Bob had mentioned—if so, Ariel could have giggled at the assortment. None of them looked too rebellious, but she was nevertheless grateful for them. Ariel couldn't believe it. She had never felt so supported and encouraged in her life.

But just as she was about to take her seat, Miles appeared at her side and handed her an envelope. He was out of breath.

"What is this?" Ariel asked, looking up at him in confusion. "Are you okay?"

"Yes. I just tried to take a copy of this to the board, but I couldn't get past some really mean, blonde lady who was guarding the table."

Ariel chuckled. "The mayor's secretary." She took the envelope from Miles.

"It's a letter from your old restaurant," Miles explained. "The Frogmore, right? I found you in their featured reviews online. I reached out to them and asked them to write a testimonial about your time there as head chef. They were more than happy to oblige, and they even mentioned the two Michelin stars the restaurant received under your leadership."

Ariel's eyes widened in surprise and gratitude as she opened and read the letter. It was filled with glowing praise for her culinary skills and leadership abilities, and it ended with a note saying that they would be thrilled to have her back at the restaurant anytime. She wasn't looking for a job, so what was she supposed to do with the letter? Tucked behind the letter was the Michelin judge's report, mentioning Ariel by name.

"Miles, this is amazing," Ariel said, looking up at him with tears in her eyes. "But how did you get this?"

"I have a friend who works at the Michelin guide," Miles said with a shrug. "From back in my company days. I guess it pays to have had a past, sometimes." He grinned. "And I thought it might help you make a stronger case to the board. Plus, I think your food deserves to be recognized by the Michelin guide, and I think it's only a matter of time before they send a judge to the B&B."

"Miles! You didn't call in a favor so that I would get starred?" Ariel's stomach turned at the thought.

"Not at all," he said, his face serious. "Did you know that all of their judges are completely anonymous? They don't even let the critics tell their families they're working for Michelin. So, none of us will know when the judge shows up. But I know you're the highest stars always, so I don't doubt you'll shine when the time comes."

"Oh," Ariel said, her cheeks flushing. "Thank you."

"No, Ariel. Thank you," Miles said, pulling her into a hug. His voice was soft in her ear. "From the first time I saw you at the harbor, it's been nothing but pure joy. Watching you in action makes me happy. And knowing that you're going to be around for a long time to come makes me smile. You've changed my life, and I … I don't really know what to say. I just wanted you to know that I'm grateful. And I'm glad we're in this together."

"Yeah," Ariel said, blinking back more tears. "I am too."

Ariel felt her heart flutter as Miles wrapped his arms around her, pulling her close. She could feel the warmth of his body and the beating of his heart as he held her. His words washed over her, and she felt a surge of emotions. Her mind was racing as she tried to process what he was saying. She could feel a smile spreading across her face as she realized that Miles was starting to have feelings for her.

She felt a sense of happiness and excitement as she hugged him back, feeling a warmth spread through her body as she basked in his embrace. It was as if all her worries and fears were melting away, and she felt like she was on top of the world.

As Miles pulled away from the hug, Ariel saw a glint—maybe even the look of love—in his eyes. His hazel gaze was intense, and it seemed like he was holding back from saying something. Ariel felt her own heart flutter with a mix of emotions; a part of her was excited by the idea of Miles having feelings for her, but another part of her was hesitant and scared. She had been hurt before and didn't want to open herself up to that possibility again. But now wasn't the time to be conflicted—she could just enjoy the excitement of what this letter might bring.

"The chefs at the Frogmore also said to tell you," Miles said, looking pleased to see her excitement, "that they're going to be sending over recipes and advice on the menu if you'd like."

Ariel nodded and wiped at the remaining tears on her cheeks. "I would love that," she said. "Thank you."

"I'm just glad to see you so happy," Miles said, his voice soft. "You deserve it."

"This letter is better than any star," Ariel said, her voice thick.

***

As the meeting began, Ariel made her case, highlighting the economic benefits of her B&B and the need for more tourism in the area. The details blurred, but she knew her lips were moving, and she was talking fast to be able to fit all of her points in during the limited time that she'd been allotted.

Ariel could feel all the eyes in the room on her. She felt clammy and hot all at the same time, and she focused on the folder she'd brought instead of on the row of board members in front of her.

"And the building has historical significance, which I plan to preserve …" She droned on, her confidence slipping. Then she was interrupted by a booming, overbearing voice from the center of the board members.

"We've heard all of this before, Miss Hawthorne. If you can't bring anything new to the proceedings, I'm afraid we've wasted our time." Mayor Stanton looked around at the other board members. "Does anyone have anything to say otherwise? You were supposed to prove added value at this meeting."

The atmosphere at the board meeting was strained, with everyone remaining quiet.

"Then, if no one has any objections, you are dismissed, Miss Hawthorne."

Ariel saw red, and her eyes blazed with anger as she confronted the mayor, her voice shaking with emotion. "You are the one," she accused, pointing an accusatory finger at him. "You set fire to my

122

house, trying to drive me out of this town and make way for your precious spa resort."

The mayor's face went pale, his eyes shifting nervously as he stumbled over his words, trying to deny Ariel's accusations. But she was relentless, her voice growing louder as she pressed him for the truth. "You think you can just bully and threaten your way into getting what you want, but you're not going to get away with it. Not this time." Her words were fierce and determined, and it was clear that she would not back down until she got the answers she was looking for.

The room was filled with a tense silence as Ariel and the mayor glared at each other, each one determined to have their way. The room erupted, everyone speaking at once with Ariel's accusation that the mayor had tried to burn down her B&B hanging in the air.

Ariel forged on. She started talking about Endless Harbor and how it had been when she was growing up, recalling the summers when she had played on the beach and swam in the bay, her face hot from the sun, her body soaked with seawater. It felt good to be home, to be back on the dock where she had first run for an incoming boat with her sister, welcoming their father home after a long day of fishing. The thought of leaving this place was too much for her to bear.

All eyes were on her, and she was shaking with anger as she addressed the room. "And lastly," she said, shouting to be heard over the din of the crowd, "Endless Harbor does not have a five-star restaurant, and I suspect that the tourists that your corporate backers are so keen to attract might like one. Luckily, I am the only Michelin-starred chef in Endless Harbor, so whose place do you think those rich tourists are going to flock to?" She held up the letter and review that Miles had brought, waving it like a flag.

As she spoke, she could see the other board members nodding in agreement. Even the mayor and his shadowy backers surely couldn't deny the logic of her argument. A gavel was beaten, the room quieted, and the assembly called for a vote.

As the board members deliberated, Ariel could hardly sit still. She was so anxious to hear their decision. She could feel the people behind her, tense and anticipating. But as the board chairman stood up to announce the verdict, Ariel held onto her sense of hope—no matter how futile it might be.

"Miss Hawthorne," the board chairman said, clearing his throat. "We have unanimously approved your proposal."

Unanimously? That meant the mayor had voted in her favor!

Ariel felt like she was on top of the world. The room erupted into cheers and applause. Katie, Charlie, Kurt, the kids, and Miles all rushed her. Ariel hugged Katie tightly, tears of joy streaming down her face. She had done it. She had gotten the approval she needed to open her B&B.

As they stepped out of the town hall, the people from the town congratulated her, and she could hear Stanton behind her, trying to spit out an improvised speech on how they would all work together to make this a success.

But she had all the success she needed, right here with her. With Katie on one side and Miles on the other, Ariel and her family walked out into the cool, coastal night.

CHAPTER TWENTY EIGHT

Ariel stopped just outside the community center when she heard her name called.

The mayor strode toward Ariel, his face red and pinched. His eyes were narrow, and his smile was a thin, hard line. Red-faced with anger and frustration, he looked as though he had aged decades in the last few minutes.

Ariel stayed composed as the mayor sauntered up to her.

"Celebrating so soon? Don't get too comfortable. This isn't finished yet."

Ariel bristled, and she held a hand out when Kurt and Miles stepped up behind her. "I'm up for a challenge. Let's start with proving you vandalized my property."

If it were possible, Stanton's face grew even redder. "Oh, you'll have it! And as for your property, I never set foot on it, and I'm not responsible for whatever happened there. But I do feel it is my responsibility to hand you this—" With that, he flourished an envelope at her, and she took it, dread settling in. She looked at the plain white envelope, almost afraid to open it. When she did, her suspicions were confirmed; it was a list of *more* necessary permits and zoning requirements for the B&B that she would need to fulfill before opening. The list was long and intimidating. Oh, she was approved for the opening, but this stack of requirements was an entirely different stack than he'd left for her with his secretary the day of their cancelled meeting. He had outmaneuvered her.

It seemed impossible for Ariel to complete this in time before the opening date. She felt like all of her hard work had been for nothing, and that she was doomed to fail before she even began.

The mayor looked at her with a smirk on his face as if he had expected nothing less than failure from her.

Ariel felt disappointed and frustrated but refused to give up just yet. She knew that somehow, some way, she'd find a way around this obstacle and make her dream come true!

"Good luck, Miss Hawthorne," Stanton said before turning to waltz away. "You're going to need it."

The mayor's words hung in the air like a thick fog. Ariel felt her stomach drop, and her heart sink into her toes. She was about to lose everything she had worked for just as quickly as it had been given to her!

Sensing her panic, Miles stepped up and put an arm around her shoulder. "Ariel," he said softly, "it's going to be okay."

The mayor scoffed, turning back to them, his face still tight with anger. "Oh really? How do you plan on fixing this?"

Miles was quick to reply. "We'll figure something out," he said confidently. He looked toward the mayor, his gaze strong and determined. "There has to be a way. We'll delay the opening, but we'll eventually get there. You can't stop us now with a little red tape."

The mayor eyed him skeptically but did not say anything else. Instead, he pointed to Ariel. "Zoning issues aren't the only problem in that little envelope. You might want to keep looking." Ariel thumbed quickly through the stack, landing on the last page—a bill for unpaid back mortgage payments, missing payments compounded with interest, and fees that now added up to thousands of dollars.

"That is current and up to date on the amount," Stanton said, sneering. "Unless you pay that off within thirty days, the house will go into foreclosure, and you'll lose it all. Too bad this was the mess daddy left you with."

Kurt moved again, this time to catch Charlie from stepping forward, ready to fight Stanton. "You slimy little …"

Ariel could feel the worry growing inside of her like a tight knot in her chest. What was she going to do? She had no idea how she was going to come up with such a large sum of money in such a short time period!

Miles, however, remained undeterred by the situation. "There are grants, loans, and organizations that will see the merit in what Ariel is trying to do."

Stanton cackled again. "Yes, but how fast will they help? Nice try, knight in shining armor, but your girlfriend's time is up."

"And what about you? You break windows and set fires. How long until the people of Endless Harbor figure out who you really are?" Ariel pressed.

Stanton stepped in close. "I've got some truth for you, Ariel. Like I said, I didn't set that fire at Leeside, and the bricks weren't me, either—in fact, they weren't even Connor. I found out that he was with his friends that night at the arcade in town until curfew."

A flicker of conflict danced across Stanton's greasy face. "Think what you will about me, Miss Hawthorne, but my son is a good boy."

Ariel's head was spinning—who had thrown the brick, and who had set the fire?

As she watched Stanton go, she began to feel dizzy. She was grateful when she felt Miles's strong arms around her, helping her back to where they had all parked their cars.

***

Rain moved in as soon as they all returned to Leeside, and Ariel felt like the skies of Maine were crying with her. After an hour of being comforted by Charlie, Kurt, and the kids, Ariel shooed them off home with the promise to call tomorrow.

Katie reluctantly went to bed, and Ariel sat with Miles in the living room, which was now much improved from when they'd sat in it the night that he'd almost kissed her. She almost longed to be back there— before she had the worry over the missed mortgage payments and the looming foreclosure. She had thought that Leeside was free and clear, and that her dad's probate years back would have found something like those missed payments before turning the house over to Charlie and Ariel.

"What do you need me to do?" Miles asked, softly rubbing her back.

"Nothing," she said. "Just be here. I'm sure things will look better in the light of day."

Miles scoffed quietly, drawing Ariel back on the couch to rest against his chest. She could hear his heartbeat, steady and soothing. "I love this about you, your optimism, but you're allowed to not be strong sometimes."

"Am I?"

Ariel started crying again, this time in big, heaving sobs. Miles just held her, let her go through the storm, her emotions matching the rage of the thunder outside. "I don't understand what's happening. The money is gone, and I'm about to lose Leeside, everything!"

"Hey, hey," he said, pulling back from her slightly. She raised her head to look at him, uncaring if she was a tearful, sweaty mess. "You have Katie, Charlie, Kurt, and the kids."

She stared at him, watching his handsome face morph through emotions. "And you have me. Listen, Ariel, I almost said it back at the board meeting, but need you to know for sure. I don't just care about you ... I—"

She sat up, her eyes flying wide. "You what?"

"I'm falling for you, Ari."

"In love?" she squeaked.

He laughed, the sound rich and warm, reaching her pained heart. "Yes, in love. I don't want to rush you into anything, but I couldn't let you sit here thinking all of your past heartache was going to end in more. Yes, there are new obstacles, and yes, we are in uncertain limbo, but you have a lot that's certain around you."

Ariel's heart skipped a beat as she heard Miles's words. She felt a warmth spread through her chest and a smile slowly spread across her face. Her eyes met his, and she saw the love shining in them. She felt her own love for him welling up inside her, and without hesitation, she threw her arms around him and whispered, "I love you too." They held each other tightly, and Ariel felt like she was home.

Miles pulled her close, and they stayed in each other's arms for a long time. When they parted, she looked into his verdant eyes, feeling a new kind of spark. With the fireplace crackling behind them, Miles lowered his head, cupped her cheek, and kissed her.

Ariel melted into the kiss, feeling all of the pent-up emotions and longing she had been holding inside finally being released. She wrapped her arms around Miles's neck, pulling him closer as their kiss deepened. She felt like her heart was going to burst with happiness as she realized she was in love with him too. The kiss was filled with the promise of a bright future together, full of love and joy. They broke the kiss, smiling at each other with tears in their eyes, happy to have found love in each other. Whatever the next few months would bring, they would face it—together.

A knock at the door interrupted the moment, and it brought Ariel to the front porch. She swung open the front door warily, visions of the kiss and the fire dancing through her mind.

"Doris!" Ariel said when her visitor came into view. "Is everything okay?"

The old woman stood nervously on the porch, wringing her hands. She gave a curt nod, her eyes roaming behind Ariel to the room beyond.

"You're actually doing it, fixing the place up," she said, though Ariel wasn't sure if it was a question or a statement. Doris's home was close enough that she had to have seen the goings-on here at Leeside, so Ariel let the words pass unanswered.

Doris sniffed the air. "Apple pie?"

"French apple tart," Ariel said, opening the door wider. She had warmed some up just an hour ago. "Would you like to come in for some?"

"No, no," Doris said, shuffling. "Only friends come in. Only family."

When she didn't speak again, Ariel frowned and held up a finger. "Stay here, Doris."

Ariel sprinted into the kitchen, past Miles and his questioning look, and rummaged the drawers, finding a plastic container with a lid that fit. She dished up a generous serving of the apple tart, drizzled it with sauce, and sealed the lid. When she returned to the porch, Doris was still there, pacing. Ariel held out the container.

"If you won't come in, take this. You'll like it."

Doris looked at the container and then at Ariel. She slowly took the offered tart. Then she lifted her chin and said, "I'm sorry. I've been snooping around. You've probably seen me."

Ariel started. "You're the lurker?"

Doris dug her furry-booted toe into the porch, twisting it in a gesture of nervousness. "I told your dad I would watch out for you if you ever came home. Or if Charlie ever moved back to the house. But the house was bad, lots of bad. Bad walls, bad floors, bad spirits."

Doris wasn't making a lot of sense, so Ariel said gently, "Did you throw the brick? And start the fire?"

Doris heaved a sigh. "I thought you should go. The bad spirits are here, loss and sadness and lies. But you didn't go after the brick. So, I smudged the house."

"Smudged?"

"Ritual fire. Cleans things up in the spiritual sense." Doris's rheumy eyes wandered the porch. "I came to say sorry. It's not my place. Maybe you like those spirits?"

Ariel almost felt relief—there was no plot to harm her or Katie. Just Doris, and whatever ghosts were guiding her. Maybe her neighbor had her own story, one with as much loss and sadness as Ariel herself. If her time here had taught her anything, with Miles and Connor and even the mayor, it was not to judge too quickly.

"Doris, I need you to not mess with the house anymore, okay? I've got this. We're getting rid of the bad by making it new again. We're going to fill it with love so that there's no more room for anything else."

She thought of Miles and what he'd just said—what they had admitted to each other—and her face warmed.

Doris nodded and smiled, revealing jagged teeth. "Good plan. I'll butt out." Then, clutching the tart closer, she turned and dashed down the porch steps. She stopped at the bottom, looking back up at Ariel. "He loved you girls so much," she said. "Don't believe the lies they tell."

Ariel nodded, despite the mystery of Doris's meaning.

A few steps out into the yard, Doris took off into a sprint, disappearing toward her house into the tall, dry grass that separated her place from Leeside.

Ariel shook her head, watching Doris go.

One mystery was solved, but so many more questions were still unanswered.

EPILOGUE

The sun shone down on the shore, and Ariel watched as Peter, Katie, and Hannah tried to get Rufus into one of Miles's rowboats. She laughed as the dog overshot the boat, landing in the still-brisk seawater. It was definitely warming up for spring, but the ocean hadn't quite gotten the message.

Kurt and Miles, behind her on the beach, tended to the clambake as Charlie looked on. Townspeople—old friends and new—were dotted along the cove, having a wonderful time. Laughter filled the air as people enjoyed appetizers set up on long tables under a nearby tree, and Ariel tried to listen to their comments of the food.

Market research.

She thought about her call with the head chef of the Frogmore earlier that day—excitement rose in her when she thought about the dishes that she was developing with Pierre, and how she would surprise Katie this summer with a trip to see the place she'd started her culinary career, if all went well with Leeside. Paris in the summer was one of the most beautiful places in the world, and Ariel wanted to continue building the stronger connection that she knew the past months had built between her and Katie. She could picture her daughter window shopping at the designer shops, and the two of them taking in art galleries and having long, leisurely lunches of fresh bread and a dozen cheeses.

Miles lifted his gaze from the clambake preparations and caught Ariel's eye. Ariel smiled, turning her head to look back at Miles. He was holding the spatula and talking to Kurt while his eyes met hers over their heads. His mossy gaze seemed to speak volumes right across the beach before he turned away with a slight smile on his lips. She dropped her eyes as warmth filled her chest. She was sure that if anyone else had noticed, they'd know exactly what had passed between them in those few seconds alone on such a beautiful day.

When she looked back up, he gave her a subtle, knowing nod before heading toward her in the sand. Every movement of his frame exuded calm composure as he made deliberate steps across the beach with a lightness that was effortless yet powerful, as though every step had been carefully considered before willed into existence. As though he were walking to her as the destination above all destinations. His eyes never changed focus away from hers until, finally, Miles reached her side, stopping just short enough to keep some space between them but close enough for conversation.

Ariel looked up at him, smiling softly as he returned her smile with equal gentleness and love in his deep, hazel eyes; they said more than any words ever could have expressed right then and there. In the past week, he had barely left her side, and they—along with her friends and family—had worked overtime to try to come up with a way to save Leeside from the looming threat of foreclosure.

It was uncertain how they would ultimately do it, but they had come far enough that Ariel had every confidence that they could weather this new storm as they had all their previous challenges.

The sun sparkled overhead, and Miles moved closer still so their arms could touch beneath a shared warmth. Like two magnets drawn together along one strong, invisible force, Ariel felt the love growing between them.

"Hey," he said.

"Hey, yourself," she replied. "When's dinner?"

He chuckled. "I'll consult the chef. Though I think he's more of a two-by-four guy than a judge of how long potatoes are supposed to cook in the ground."

"That's okay," Ariel said, leaning her head on his shoulder. "On second thought, I don't even need food. I could just stay here with you and be perfectly happy for the rest of my life."

Miles grinned and took her hand.

They were not out of the woods yet with the house, Ariel knew. Her father was still missing, and she had a crazy neighbor who spoke in riddles and had set fire to her bushes. Stanton might continue to be a thorn in her side for the rest of her days in Endless Harbor. But no matter what happened today or tomorrow or even next year, nothing would change how special this moment was already becoming between her and Miles—and nothing would change the newfound sense of home and new purpose that she had found since returning to the sea.

Her thoughts turned to her father. It was a funny thing, to be thinking of him now when his memory was so painful. But it wasn't pain she felt now. It was understanding. She didn't understand why he'd left—if he had—but she understood that everything in life had layers, and that nothing was what it seemed on the surface. She let go of the anger that she felt when she thought of his absence. There wasn't any space anymore for judging. She felt at peace, at least for the moment, with the uncertainty of what had happened with Lee Briggs in the past.

Her gaze followed the stones around the cove toward the lighthouse, watching as Hannah chased Rufus down the beach, only to return with the dog chasing her in search of indulgent, loving petting.

Miles slipped his hand free of hers and reached down, pulling up a small piece of pebble from the sandy beach. He held it out to her on his palm and looked up into her eyes. "Hey, look at this."

Ariel gasped and looked at his palm. The small object that lay there was a tiny shape made of polished shell, smoothed by the waves in a way that looked perfect—a little, shell heart that connected the beauty of the sea with how she was feeling in this moment.

Her eyes flashed up to Miles. She barely knew what she was doing as she reached out and planted a kiss on his lips before throwing her arms around him and dragging him into her lap. They had been careful to keep their budding relationship low-key, but here, surrounded by the people she loved most, Ariel was ready to let it go.

She heard wolf whistles behind them, and Katie exclaimed, "Gross!"

Miles laughed. "You haven't seen anything yet," he told the onlookers.

He kissed Ariel again, and she nearly forgot where they were as she lost herself in him. But just before they got too carried away, he drew away with a smile and helped her to her feet before wrapping an arm around her waist.

The sun sank quickly as the sky took on a vibrant mixture of oranges, pinks, and purples with the intensity of a gorgeous sunset; it set aglow the white sand and green-blue water around them in a dazzling play of light and color.

"This is perfect," she said, sinking back down to the sand as Miles did the same. "No matter what happens with Leeside, nothing will ever be able to take this moment away from me. There is no place I would rather be or anyone I would rather spend it with than right here, right now, and with you and my family."

Miles studied her for a long moment, taking both of her hands in his and bringing them to his lips. He met her eyes with an intensity that almost made her blush once more before repeating a single word in a whisper that only she could hear—a whisper that promised his love "Forever."

As they stood there, hand in hand, watching the sun dip lower on the horizon, Ariel couldn't help but feel grateful for the journey that had led her to this point. She had come to Endless Harbor to start over, to rebuild her life and her daughter's, and through the challenges and setbacks, she had found love, family, and a sense of belonging that she had never known before. Even in her childhood, though there had been happy times in Maine, but she hadn't known enough, experienced enough, to appreciate true happiness—hard-won and fought for, pursued despite any and all odds stacked against her.

Ariel knew that there were still obstacles to overcome, but with Miles by her side, and her family at her back, she felt more than capable of facing them head on. She looked up at Miles, her heart full of love and hope for the future, and he smiled down at her, his eyes shining with the same emotions. They stayed there for a moment longer, lost in the beauty of the moment before rising from the sand, together.

NOW AVAILABLE!

ALWAYS, FOREVER
(Endless Harbor—Book 2)

In a new sweet romance series by #1 Bestseller Fiona Grace, Summer is coming for this small town in Maine, and with it the hopeful opening of Charlotte Rose's B&B. But small-town life in Maine is a shock for Miami-transplant Charlotte Rose and her teenage daughter. Renovating a house for the first time is an even bigger shock. But nothing is as unexpected as the new love that walks into her life. Can he the one?

"Wow, this book takes off & never stops! I couldn't put it down! Highly recommended for those who love a great mystery with twists, turns, romance, and a long lost family member! I am reading the next book right now!"
--Amazon reviewer (regarding *Murder in the Manor*)

"Wish all books were this good a mystery romance and love. Did not want to stop reading this book—loved it."
--Amazon reviewer (regarding *Murder in the Manor*)

ALWAYS, FOREVER is book #2 in a new series by #1 bestselling author Fiona Grace, whose books have received over 10,000 five-star reviews and ratings.

A charming sweet romance series will transport you to another world, the ENDLESS HARBOR series will make you laugh, make you cry, will keep you turning pages late into the night—and will make you fall in love with romance all over again. A page-turner packed with jaw-dropping twists, it is impossible to put down!

Future books in the series are also available.

"The story line wasn't just a who done it, but had a story about her life and romance, including village life. Very entertaining."
--Amazon reviewer (regarding *Murder in the Manor*)

"It has endearing and sometimes quirky characters, a plot that keeps you reading and the right amount of romance. I can't wait to start book two!"
--Amazon reviewer (regarding *Murder in the Manor*)

"What a great story of murder, romance, new beginnings, love, friend ships and a wonderful cascade of mystery."
--Amazon reviewer (regarding *Murder in the Manor*)

Fiona Grace

Fiona Grace is author of the LACEY DOYLE COZY MYSTERY series, comprising nine books; of the TUSCAN VINEYARD COZY MYSTERY series, comprising seven books; of the DUBIOUS WITCH COZY MYSTERY series, comprising three books; of the BEACHFRONT BAKERY COZY MYSTERY series, comprising six books; of the CATS AND DOGS COZY MYSTERY series, comprising nine books; of the ELIZA MONTAGU COZY MYSTERY series, comprising five books (and counting); and of the ENDLESS HARBOR ROMANTIC COMEDY series, comprising five books (and counting).

Fiona would love to hear from you, so please visit www.fionagraceauthor.com to receive free ebooks, hear the latest news, and stay in touch.

SKEPTIC IN SALEM: AN EPISODE OF DEATH (Book #3)

BEACHFRONT BAKERY COZY MYSTERY
BEACHFRONT BAKERY: A KILLER CUPCAKE (Book #1)
BEACHFRONT BAKERY: A MURDEROUS MACARON (Book #2)
BEACHFRONT BAKERY: A PERILOUS CAKE POP (Book #3)
BEACHFRONT BAKERY: A DEADLY DANISH (Book #4)
BEACHFRONT BAKERY: A TREACHEROUS TART (Book #5)
BEACHFRONT BAKERY: A CALAMITOUS COOKIE (Book #6)

CATS AND DOGS COZY MYSTERY
A VILLA IN SICILY: OLIVE OIL AND MURDER (Book #1)
A VILLA IN SICILY: FIGS AND A CADAVER (Book #2)
A VILLA IN SICILY: VINO AND DEATH (Book #3)
A VILLA IN SICILY: CAPERS AND CALAMITY (Book #4)
A VILLA IN SICILY: ORANGE GROVES AND VENGEANCE (Book #5)
A VILLA IN SICILY: CANNOLI AND A CASUALTY (Book #6)

Made in the USA
Las Vegas, NV
06 May 2024